"Ambush!"

Enemy gunfire and the clanging of bullets finding their target quickly drowned out the roar of the helicopter. Lyons turned and at that moment, in the glow of the chopper's instrument panel, the Ironman saw the pilot's head come apart.

Lyons had witnessed head shots before, but he was not prepared to see the abrupt stiffening of the body as nerves overloaded, galvanizing the muscles into rigidity; the snapping sideways of the head from the force of the impact; and the look of panic that glazed the pilot's eyes as he thought of all the things he had left unfinished.

At the pilot's spasm, the chopper made a wild lurch to one side. It twisted and then dropped the remaining few feet to the ground, striking the rocky surface in a bone-jarring crash.

As the dust settled an eerie silence invaded Death Valley.

Mack Bolan's

ABLE TEAM

HIT AND RUN

Dick Stivers

A GOLD EAGLE BOOK FROM

WORLDWIDE

TORONTO • NEW YORK • LONDON • PARIS
AMSTERDAM • STOCKHOLM • HAMBURG
ATHENS • MILAN • TOKYO • SYDNEY

First edition June 1987

ISBN 0-373-61230-3

Special thanks and acknowledgment to
Chuck Rogers for his contribution to this work.

Printed in Canada

PROLOGUE

"How about Denver? I've never been to Denver. Might be kind of fun to see that city."

"Nah. Denver sucks."

"How do you know that?"

"Used to live there. In the summer it's fucking hot and dirty, and in the winter it's fucking cold and dirty. Even the snow is dirty in Denver."

"Oh."

"Yeah. Trust me. We don' wanna do Denver. Any place but Denver."

"No shit. I always heard Denver was pretty sharp. How come it's got such a great rep if it's so bad, then?"

"Who knows? Maybe 'cause of their falls."

"No shit? They have mondo falls in Denver?"

"Of course, you asshole. They have falls everywhere. What the fuck you talkin' about, anyway?"

"Falls like Old Faithful, man? Niagara Falls and shit?"

"No, no *waterfalls*, you dick brain. Falls. You know. Like autumns. Right after summer and before winter. Autumns, man. Falls. Leaves dropping off trees. That kinda falls."

"Oh."

"Besides, Old Faithful ain't a waterfall anyway. It's a geyser or some shit. Anyway, that's gotta be why Denver has such a big rep. Their falls. Autumn is real nice in Denver. Trees turnin' different colors and shit."

"All right. Maybe we'll do Denver this fall."

"We'll do Denver if I say we do Denver. And we'll do it when I say, and how I say. And if I say we don't ever do Denver, we ain't never gonna do Denver."

"All right, G.M. Be cool, man. You're the boss, G.M. We do wherever you say we do."

"Fuckin-A right I'm the boss."

The two men fell silent. Two others looked on. Finally one of them spoke again.

"So where we gonna go, G.M., anyway? I mean, where do you want us to go?"

"Let me think, Slimy. You hear me? Jes' let me think a goddamn minute, will ya?"

"Sure, G.M., sure. Whatever you say, man."

A few moments later the man called G.M.—the initials stood for Garbage Mouth—spoke up again. At six-four, he was a massively muscled, hairy beast with small, piglike eyes that burned in his bearded face.

"I like L.A.," he said at last.

Slimy looked dubious. "I dunno, G.M. L.A. cops are some mean dudes. Maybe we oughta try some other place besides L.A."

"Fuck the L.A. cops. I ain't afraid a no L.A. pigs."

"I'm tellin' ya, G.M., them guys play for keeps. Like, super hardball, you know? They'd just as soon kill you as look at you. I ain't too keen on L.A."

"How many guys you killed, Slimy?"

"Huh?"

"You heard me. How many guys have you fucking killed, dick brain?"

"Me, personally? Or how many have I helped you guys with?"

"Either way."

Slimy thought for a few moments. "Eleven, I guess. Or was it ten? No, eleven, counting that broad that had the heart attack when you were banging her. So maybe make it ten for me personally, plus the broad. Not countin' Nam, a course."

"That include that kid that suffocated when we left him tied up? That redheaded little bastard?"

"Okay. Twelve then, counting him. But he doesn't really count, in a way. That was more accidental, actually. Like that broad. Call it ten guys I really killed, plus a coupla 'accidentals.'"

"Law don't call it accidental." Both Slimy and G.M. looked at the man who had spoken. Up until then he had been content to watch and listen to the exchange between Slimy and G.M.

The voice sounded as if it came from the pits of hell, or from a grave at the very least. Dead. Without inflection or intonation of any sort. Just a flat, deep, mechanical monotone, like a speaking computer set on "low" and "slow."

The man who owned the voice looked immense and dead. He was six-five and big the way a whale is big—huge and hard but without any particular shape or distinguishing features. His skin was a dead-fish white. Even his head was shiny and bald, and for some reason it never got tanned or burned.

But the man's most striking features didn't come from nature; they had been added by prison needle and prison ink. Or, to be more precise, only the early ones had been added by prison materials. For those that came later—and that accounted for most of them now—had been done on the outside.

On his right shoulder a tattooed skull grinned out at the world.

It had been applied in vivid detail and was located on the outside of his deltoid, the cap of muscle that went around the point of his shoulder.

The skull looked outward from a dark blue-black patch. It had been a sophisticated project even for tattoos—the actual skull itself was the man's own stark white skin, set off against the dark background. Rather than drawing and inking the skull into the skin, the tattooist had inked out everything around it, leaving the white flesh for the death's-head figure. The details, of course—the eye sockets, jaw-bone, teeth—had been supplied by dark lines where appropriate.

Most tattoos looked lurid. These looked stark and macabre, resulting in a startling impact of evil and death.

Below the tattoo on the deltoid reposed another skull, done in the same fashion, white on a blue-black spot some three inches by three inches. This one was on the outside of the arm. In total, a series of seven death's-heads ran down the white flesh to the wrist.

A similar chain ran up the outside of the huge man's left arm. This chain, however, had one fewer than the right; a single space remained just above the left wrist. It was ready and waiting.

Yet another skull ran across the man's immense back, connecting the two chains.

One skull per victim.

Kill somebody, add another tattoo, like Boy Scout merit badges, military campaign ribbons or notches on a fictional gunslinger's six-shooter.

Some of the skulls had red lips. Most did not.

The red-lipped ones stood for women. Up until recently he had killed more men than women. Lately, however, he had been reversing that trend.

Yet despite this death's-head display, the mark that earned his name was something quite different. Due to the man's mastadonlike size, it wasn't readily apparent unless he tipped his head forward, so that his own eyes looked straight down.

A single 8—tattooed in jet black—ran from front to back on the top of his skull.

It resembled to some extent the negative of an eight ball, which of course would normally be black with the figure set off in white or on a white spot.

Even G.M., as the leader of the group, feared this huge man.

"That's true," he agreed. "Law don't call it accidental. You kill somebody during a burglary or a robbery, even if you weren't trying to kill 'em, it's first degree."

The pale monstrous man with the dead voice nodded his head. "First degree all the way."

A fourth voice interjected, singing out the words in a tuneless melody.

"First degree, first degree
First degree for thee and me."

G.M. glanced at the fourth member, a lean, dark, sinewy man with the strange, intense, not-quite-right eyes of a psychopath. He was of average height, but had such transparent skin and so little body fat that he looked as if he had been skinned for a medical exhibit. The long and wiry muscles of his arms were interwoven with prominent veins. His shoulders and chest were equally muscular, the effect being one of knotty clumps of gristle sprouting from his frame.

"Right on, Whip," G.M. said grinning. "We're in this together. Any one of us falls, we all fall."

"Ring around the dead man
Eight Ball broke his head, man.
Murder, murder, we all fall down."

Whip's voice made a mincing parody of "Ring around the Rosy." The huge man sporting the skulls down his arm and the digit on his cranium nodded at this reference to his immense strength, a slow grin spreading across his face. He liked it when Whip said nice things about him, especially in a song.

In prison Whip had been nicknamed Psycho.

He'd been convicted of second-degree murder and sentenced to life in prison. Then, in the late 1970s, the California legislature had overhauled the penalty provisions of the entire penal code. In a burst of goodwill, they had made it so that anybody convicted of second degree could be out in five to seven years.

The law's the law, and those inside doing life for second degree were allowed to take advantage of this legislative largess.

That included Psycho and a hell of a lot of others. It provided a temporary easing of the overcrowding of the prison population and saved the taxpayers the expense of more prisons. Or postponed it, anyway. The legislature increased the penalty a couple of years later, but for Psycho it was like landing on Chance and drawing a Get Out of Jail Free card.

He was still on parole of course—society had to be protected. And his parole agent, a tough-minded but hopelessly overworked ex-police officer, followed through with the prison board's specifications that Psycho receive counseling once a month at a state clinic as a condition of his parole.

Psycho promised he would, and he was as good as his word.

The counselor at the clinic was a young woman named Valentine Fitzer. She was an adjustment counselor I, a rookie counselor.

Valentine took her job seriously. She had majored in social sciences at a junior college, and she knew how important one's self-image was to one's behavior. And a name could have a profound effect on that self-image, therefore indirectly affecting behavior. Accordingly, she suggested that Psycho's readjustment to society might be made easier if he chose a new nickname.

"Pick one that doesn't seem so, well, negative," Valentine told him. "One that will be a more positive expression of your outward 'self' as well as your inward abilities," she explained.

Psycho nodded earnestly and began trying to find an appropriate moniker. After all, it was a condition of his parole, and he intended to abide by those conditions, at least some of them. But maybe not the more onerous ones, such as "Don't kill any more people," "Don't violate any other laws," or "Must seek or maintain full-time employment."

Finding a suitable nickname wasn't easy.

Valentine didn't like most of the ones he liked. And they were good, solid names, too, names such as Animal, Freako, Mutant, Dog, Wild Man, Bongo-bongo and Killer.

"Those all just sound too negative," she informed him.

So Psycho kept looking for a suitable label, all the while wondering how it would feel to wrap the plaited coils of his bullwhip around the pale, soft neck of the little adjustment counselor I who was giving him such a hassle, how he'd choke the living hell out of her . . .

Then he had it. Inspiration struck. Valentine had been right all along, because from the frustration of this adversity came inspiration. The very image of what he would like to do to her became what he had been searching for.

Whip.

He told her, and the earnest little adjustment counselor I agreed with it because it sounded sharp and snappy. And even Psycho—or Whip—had to agree that it sounded much less negative than any of the others.

So Psycho became Whip.

In several ways the nickname was perfect. After all, he liked bullwhips; in fact, he carried one everywhere he went, coiled like a lasso and hung on the belt that supported his filthy blue jeans. Also, because his physique was so long and lean, the name indeed made an accurate expression of his outward "self." Moreover, it didn't do too badly as an expression of his inward abilities, either, because that was what he liked to do to the prostitutes that he would occasionally kidnap and, in his words, "Pleasure."

"Hey, that's pretty good, Psycho—I mean, Whip," acknowledged G.M. If it hadn't been that Whip made such a useful tool, and was so loyal to G.M., the leader would have snapped his wiry neck a long time ago. "You're real quick with a song, that's for sure."

Whip beamed, then quickly turned his head away and looked downward so that nobody would see how happy he was that he had pleased his master.

G.M. turned back to Slimy and continued to discredit the latter's thesis regarding the toughness of the LAPD.

"Okay, Slimy. Make it ten guys you killed, not counting Nam. And me, I done twice that many at least. And Eight Ball and Psy—uh—Whip, they each done well over a dozen."

"Sixteen," rumbled Eight Ball. "Number seventeen at bat, eighteen on deck and nineteen in the hole."

For his part, Whip just nodded.

"So?" Slimy responded to G.M.

"So you think there's a single, solitary, fucking L.A. cop alive that's wasted twelve guys? Even one shit-for-brains pig that comes close to any of us?"

Slimy thought that over. "No, I guess not."

"You better believe there's not."

"So what's your point?"

"My point, Slimy, my lad, is this. We—me, you, Eight Ball and Whip—we're the baddest assholes around. We're ten times badder than a whole platoon of Los Angeles pigs. Believe it, and believe it fucking good."

"I believe it, G.M."

The leader continued. "Besides, we got the guns, right?"

"Right on."

"We got the guts, right?"

"Yeah. I mean, right on."

"We got the experience, right?"

This time Slimy didn't say anything.

"I mean, Eight Ball's a fucking black belt, for Christ's sake. He can put his head through a steel plate and come out smilin'. And Whip. That fucker can blow up anything on this earth. Give that bastard a little C-4 and some det cord, and he'll turn the fucking great pyramids into the great craters."

G.M. paused, then continued. "And you, you shoot like an ace. Ain't no weapon alive you can't make play a Dixie waltz if you want to."

"Plus the knife," Slimy reminded him. "Don't forget about the knife."

"Yeah, yeah. Plus the knife. You're a bad man with a blade, Slimy. That's for sure. Almost as bad as me. And, long as we're talking about it, look at me. I'm two-forty this week, I deadlift eight hundred pounds, and I can shoot a fucking M-16 in each hand. Any L.A. pig tries to get in the way, we'll rip his head off and shit in his goddamn lungs."

"Yeah, you're right, G.M. L.A.'d be good, all right."

"And we got one other thing, too."

G.M. paused and waited for emphasis. Little white flecks of spittle gathered at the corners of his mouth. His eyes blazed with the fire of drugs and fanaticism. Then he continued, his voice raspy and tense.

"We like it. We like our work, Slimy. We like takin' those fat-cat bastards and rat-fucking them right where it hurts. We flat fucking *like* it. And because of that, we're good at it."

"Right on, G.M."

"And no little LAPD piggies gonna stop us."

"No way, G.M. No way at all." Slimy knew when to back off.

"Good. L.A. it is, then. You like that, Slimy?"

"I like it."

"You, Eight Ball? Whip?" G.M. looked at his other two killers.

The two men looked at each other and exchanged nods. Then Eight Ball spoke up for both of them. "We like it."

"Good. We do L.A. next week."

1

"Shit, I just can't figure it out."

Gene leaned back in his swivel chair and surveyed the mass of papers before him. His dismay and disgust were apparent.

"Problem?" Carl Lyons asked, his voice indicating concern.

The two men were sitting in the office of Paul's Gym, which Gene owned. His full name was Eugene Paul, and he'd been lifting weights ever since he'd gotten out of the army twenty-five years ago. Today, at age fifty plus, he sported eighteen-inch arms and the ability to do a strict barbell curl with two hundred pounds on any given day.

Even in the current fitness craze, a two-hundred-pound curl was virtually unheard of.

Most people trained on machines, showed off their little custom-made workout suits and tried to hit on the members of the opposite—or same—sex who appealed to them. They did this at fancy spas and fitness complexes, many of which had more franchises than McDonald's.

What those people didn't do, as a rule, was lift any real weights.

Not that that was necessarily bad. For people—especially business executives and women—who only wanted conditioning and toning and who didn't care about being really strong—the fitness complexes had some advantages.

Certainly they were a lot better than nothing. Still, the only thing that most men who trained at those places could do with two hundred pounds on an Olympic bar was to roll it along the floor.

Maybe. Provided they warmed up real well first.

Gene Paul wasn't like that. "Someday I'll get back into serious training," he would lament. "Get back to something close to where I used to be."

"So what's the problem?" Carl Lyons repeated. At just a little under six feet, Lyons's weight hovered between a hundred and ninety and two hundred, all of it lean and solid. When he was lifting heavy himself, Lyons weighed as much as two hundred and ten to two hundred and fifteen. If he laid off for a while, or worked on some other form of exercise, or was in the middle of a mission, his weight might go as low as a hundred and eighty-five.

Ditto if he was in the hospital recuperating from bullet wounds or whatever other violent, and painful, damage his body had sustained in the line of duty.

On this particular day he was closer to a hundred and ninety, lean, but still strong in the way that rawhide was strong—hard, tough and durable.

Although he had studied several forms of martial arts at one time or another in his life—notably aikido and tae kwon do, two vastly different forms—Lyons had never pursued the black belt. Nonetheless, much of his strength, and toughness, came from what was generally touted as the ultimate goal of martial arts—a toughness of mind.

Inner hard, he called it—to be distinguished from the other kind of hard. Lyons had that inner hard, that toughness of mind. He also got that other kind, too, on appropriate occasions.

He had been born with a healthy dose of whatever it took to have that toughness. As a cop on the LAPD, he had developed it by o.j.t., "on the job training." That meant tempering it the hard way—on the streets.

As a cop, Lyons had never shirked or shied away from responding to the radio calls in the tough areas where he worked.

"Two-forty-five in progress at Hank's Chili Bar, possibly six suspects involved, pool cues and broken bottles, no further details. Any unit in the area please respond," the radio would inform them in those days.

"Two-forty-five" was the code for assault with a deadly weapon.

Lyons had learned very quickly why some cops drove slowly to those calls. Hell, it sometimes happened that other cops—only a few in those days—didn't even hear the radio. Must have been in a "blind spot" when that call had gone out; one of those pockets where the radio signal didn't reach effectively.

Sure.

Just try walking into good old Hank's relying on the badge and the uniform to make people come to order. See how far it got you when it turned out that the "two-forty-five" actually consisted of three massive hard-hat types—steelworkers, truck drivers, dockhands—going fist city with a like number of outlaw bikers.

Whatever was behind those calls, Lyons had never shirked them. He'd hit the toggle switch to turn on the overhead red and blue lights, grab the mike—"Forty-two-Zebra responding, Code 3," meaning red lights—and haul ass all the way. Usually he would be the first officer on the scene.

Incidents such as that also taught him something else about human nature.

He saw how quickly those five or six good Americans joined sides with one another, seeing eye to eye instead of going fist to eye, when they had a common enemy in the form of a cop whose job it was to break up the fight.

No, the uniform and badge didn't help then. And the side arm—a .38 Police Special in those days—didn't help either; it wasn't a deadly force situation. Not yet, anyway.

It was kick ass and take names. Or get your own kicked.

There was only one thing to do, he knew, assuming you were going to be a cop who handled the calls instead of ducking them. Just nut up and do it. Do it scared if you had to, but just fucking do it, with the gravel in your guts and the wind in your fists.

Physical toughness was essential of course. But even that only went so far. What carried the day and sent the bad guys to jail instead of the good guy to the hospital was the mental attitude.

Lyons had it. And, like his physical muscles, his mind grew harder and tougher the more he tested it.

Add to that toughness a number of sporadic episodes of martial arts training as the years went by—six months here, eight months there. Add to that a lot of specialized training in other combative endeavors at the expense of Uncle Sam, most of it secret, all of it job-related. Then throw the man into the pit where the fires of hell itself burned, and the result was the Carl Lyons of today.

Case-hardened.

Even Gene Paul didn't know all of it, just as Lyons didn't know about all of the escapades Gene had survived while a member of Special Forces. But the rugged blond man with the cold blue eyes who now lounged in Gene's office was one of the world's foremost counterterrorist experts.

A killer.

Or, to be more precise, an assassin, a lone wolf whose only concession to the human animal's tendency to band together was Able Team.

The core of Able Team consisted of himself and two friends, Rosario "Politician" Blancanales and Hermann "Gadgets" Schwarz. And, in a more general sense, Able Team included Stony Man Farm, hidden in the Blue Ridge Mountains just a chopper-hopper from Washington, D.C., from which Lyons and the others operated.

Stony Man wasn't actually a division of the United States government, of course, not like the CIA or the FBI or the NSA. The Stony Man operation was sanctioned by the President himself. Its existence wasn't common knowledge—Hal Brognola wanted it that way.

Brognola acted as the Chief of Operations for Stony Man. He was a former specialist with the Justice Department in the area of covert operations, where he had served for many years before joining Stony Man. And, as a result of that experience, Brognola had those special resources—it was a kind of "currency" actually—that were all-important in the secret world.

Contacts.

Brognola had contacts.

Actually, in that respect, the secret world was no different than the everyday world of business and commerce. To get things done one had to have contacts. It didn't matter whether the setting was running a real estate agency or a construction company, or running a drug ring, or running teams of counterterrorist operatives. Contacts were a must.

As a result of Brognola's contacts—all of whom were discreet and included people at the highest and most sensitive levels of government—Stony Man increasingly got called in on cases where the CIA or Delta Force couldn't be used.

Maybe the job was one where the government couldn't be linked in any way to what was done, one where the team could be disavowed if things didn't work out. Maybe it was a case where the dirty work that had to be done simply didn't fit within any of the charters of even the most flexible of those official groups. And maybe the case was just so dirty—the odds so great against success—that Stony Man alone would undertake it.

That was where Able Team fitted in, especially in the area of combating domestic terrorist activities, or at least handling the stateside aspects of those groups.

Carl Lyons, the brash former LAPD officer, blond and rugged, a loner, champion of the cause of the victims who couldn't protect themselves from their predators.

Rosario Blancanales, aka Politician, because of his easy charm and quick smile, a stocky ex-Black Beret, the son of illegal immigrants—wetbacks, as they were called in those days—who had fought in Vietnam and was still fighting.

Hermann "Gadgets" Schwarz, who had also served in Nam, an electronics and computer genius with a flair for both the mechanical and the metaphysical, but a killer himself nonetheless.

If any of them—Lyons, Blancanales, Schwarz or their colleagues in Delta Force or Blue Light or any one of the various commando units around the world—ever thought about it, they would agree that facing death was their life, both in terms of what they did and in terms of why they did it.

And, if those same men were truly candid about those thoughts, they would admit that someday their commitment would be their death as well.

Lyons understood those things, just as he understood that he was something of a loner. And he accepted them. It didn't bother him to be the lone wolf, and it didn't bother him particularly to know that he was laying his ass on the proverbial line for people he didn't even know, or who didn't know he existed.

He knew also that being a loner had certain practical advantages, notably that there would be fewer innocent bystanders in the field of fire if somebody tried to take him out, permanently.

Lyons knew. Something like that had happened before. And, as long as he was down here, he would take some flowers to the grave.

Gene, however, was one of the exceptions to the Carl Lyons lone-wolf rule. Not only was he eminently capable of taking care of himself, but he and Lyons saw eye to eye on a lot of things. And this included things they didn't talk about as well as those they did.

"So what's the problem?" Lyons repeated.

Gene waved a piece of paper at him. Lyons recognized it as a bill, then saw the blue graphics logo that bore the letters S D G & E. The initials stood for San Diego Gas and Electric, widely regarded as one of the most expensive utility companies in the country.

"What's that?" Lyons asked.

"My fucking electricity bill." As he held up the bill, a vein on his bicep stood out in sharp relief.

The Ironman nodded sympathetically. "Yeah, I hear what you're sayin'."

"I mean," continued the weight lifter, "I just can't see how it could be this high for one month. Shit, I don't have enough appliances in this whole place to use up that much juice."

"How much is it?"

"Six hundred fucking dollars. Well," he amended, "five hundred and ninety-two, to be exact."

Lyons eyebrows narrowed sharply. "That *is* high."

"Yeah, and I haven't even been running the air-conditioners. This can't be right." He shook his head grimly, then looked at Lyons. "You know anything about electricity?"

"It makes lights light. It shocks you if you touch it. It's been used to kill convicted murderers. That's about it. Why?"

Gene was only half listening to Lyons's recital and social commentary. "I wonder if there's such a thing as an electricity leak," he mused. "Like a partial short, or grounding, or something. Maybe that's what's going on."

Lyons, wondering if he could kid Gene out of his mood, continued. "Come to think of it, I used to know some electricity jokes, too. I wish I could remember them. You'd probably get a charge out of 'em. Not that they're that great, but they're not too shocking at least."

Gene looked up and rolled his eyes disgustedly, but said nothing.

"It's kinda like democracy," Lyons continued. "You know, one man, one volt."

"Yeah. Well, this one man couldn't have used all these volts. Or watts, or whatever the hell they're charging me up the ass for."

"All right, all right," said Lyons with a good-natured grin. "You don't like my jokes, so I'll just go ohm."

"Watt's the problem, you guys?" a new voice chimed in. "Something wrong? Just keep plugging away—you'll get it wired sooner or later."

The voice belonged to Gene Paul, Jr. or Gene-O, as he was usually called. At age twenty-eight, Gene-O stood six feet and weighed an even one-ninety. Unlike his father, who was addicted to working out, Gene-O had a love/hate relationship with the weights. He would train hard for a while, then not touch a barbell for months. A welder and machine shop artisan by profession, he'd pass for the Marlboro cowboy in welding togs.

Wordlessly Gene waved the bill at his son. Gene-O examined it and let out a low whistle. "Holy shit!"

"Well," proclaimed Gene, "it just can't be right. That's all there is to it."

"Unless somebody is ripping us off," Gene-O suggested.

Lyons suddenly came to attention. The ex-cop in him liked the sound of what Gene-O had said.

He had been sitting there trying to construct a single sentence with three electricity puns in it. He had come up with one that used both "currently" and "switch," but working a third one in had him stumped. The only other term he could come up with was "amp," but it didn't lend itself readily to punning. Too bad, he thought. That would have been the coup de grace.

"I wonder if somebody *is* ripping you off," he said eagerly. "Let's go take a look."

Wordlessly the three men got up and trooped up the hill from Gene's office to the gym itself.

The neighborhood, an older part of town, consisted of a mixture of residences and commercial structures. The area was in a state of flux—some of the places were well maintained or in the process of being renovated, others were in decay. Immediately adjacent to the gym on one side was a nice home. On the other side stood a shabby neighborhood bar, behind which was a dilapidated residential duplex.

The bar and duplex were separated from that side of the gym by about twelve to fifteen feet. That distance wasn't usable as an alley, and anyway there was nothing to get to behind the gym except more of Gene's property. As a result, he had allowed shrubbery to grow there as a sort of impromptu hedge between his business and the adjacent structures.

The three men circled the gym, then pushed through the bushes, Gene in the lead.

Suddenly he stopped in his tracks. "Well, I'll be a son of a bitch."

"What is it?" Gene-O inquired of his father.

Gene pointed.

An orange construction-grade extension cord—capable of handling a lot of amps—lay before them. It came from the window of a little-used storage room in the gym. One corner of the screen had been bent, and Lyons could see where the aluminum frame had buckled. The window itself was open about three-eighths of an inch, just enough to accommodate the thickness of the cord.

The three men followed the cord with their eyes. It trailed down the wall, went into the bushes and disappeared in the direction of the run-down duplex.

Gene pushed the bushes carefully aside and made his way through them, following the orange cord.

It was an easy trail.

The cord led straight to the duplex and into a window on the side nearest them. Unlike the window at the gym, through which the thieves had gained access to Gene's power, this one had been completely shattered. Cheap print curtains hung over it from the inside. Rock music issued from the opening.

"Well, I'll be a son of a bitch," Gene repeated. "Those bastards *are* ripping me off."

"Looks like it," Lyons agreed. "You know who's staying here?" he asked Gene.

The gym owner shrugged. "I've seen a few of them in the parking lot, I guess. Biker types. Probably drug dealers, but basically lowlifes, not even enough balls to be real bikers."

"Think we ought to call the cops?" Gene-O asked.

It was Lyons who responded. "We could do that," he said, using a tone of voice that clearly said, "But we shouldn't."

"Think they'd do anything?"

The Ironman shook his head. "Nope."

"Why not?" Gene's voice was outraged.

"First of all, they'd need a search warrant to get inside the house. And they won't want to make the effort to get one, even if a judge and D.A. would do it."

"Why would they need a search warrant?" asked Gene-O.

"This is California, man. Best place in the world to be a crook. With a couple of exceptions, the appellate courts suck eggs. If the courts made cars, reverse is the only gear they'd install. Take it from me, you'd need a warrant."

"And even then, probably nothing would happen to them," observed Gene disgustedly.

Lyons nodded. "The jerks would get some public defender appointed to defend them. Which you, as a taxpayer, pay for. Then they'd say that none of them knew anything about the cord."

"How could they say that?"

"I've seen it happen. They'd blame it on some phantom probably." Lyons changed his voice to a sniveling whine. "'Jeez, your honor, I don't know nothing about it. There was this other guy, see, who stayed here for a while, and he must've done it, 'cause he told us the power was all okay, and that he paid the bill, and stuff, and no, I haven't seen him for quite a while, snivel, snivel, whine, whine.'" Lyons changed back to a normal tone. "You get my drift?" he asked.

Gene-O shook his head. "And a judge would buy that shit?"

"Probably. And if one of them did get convicted, he'd probably blame it on a bad childhood. Society's fault. He was just trying to get attention or something. I had a case back on the PD where a dirtbag little dipshit stabbed his nine-year-old brother, and the judge gave him probation because he was just making a plea for help. The guy wasn't that little, either. Seventeen, in fact.''

"What a bunch of shit."

"You got that right."

Lyons, who thought he had by and large come to grips with the fact that there wasn't much justice in the world, was surprised at the old anger he felt. The crooks skated, and as usual, it was the ordinary guy, the decent Joe, who paid the price of the courts' impotence.

The three men fell silent. They stood there in the heat, gazing at the extension cord that was piping Gene's electricity into the duplex.

At that point, a window air conditioner in the duplex clattered to life.

Gene looked at his son and his friend. "I don't even run my own air conditioner," he said softly. "It costs too much. And these creeps take a heavy-duty cord and run theirs off me."

Lyons looked around, his eyes scanning the ground for a tool or implement of some sort, or for an inspiration. He wasn't wearing a weapon, but the day he needed one to handle a bunch of pseudo-biker drug dealers would be the day he quit Able Team and took up knitting.

Or maybe crocheting. Though, come to think of it, he really didn't know the difference between the two.

The area surrounding the house was littered with junk and old car parts that were half hidden by the weeds that grew stubbornly out of the oily dirt. No inspiration there.

Then Lyons spied a massive chunk of iron lying on the ground. It was the cylinder head off an old engine. It had probably belonged to a truck or tractor originally. Lyons had worked on his share of cars in his time, and this cylinder head looked bigger than any he could recall.

He bent down and gave a yank to dislodge it from the dirt and debris. The head came free, and he heaved it up to his chest. He estimated that it weighed eighty or ninety pounds.

"What're you going to do?" asked Gene-O softly.

"That judge was right," Lyons responded cryptically.

"What do you mean?"

"They're just trying to get our attention."

Gene-O looked puzzled, but his father caught Lyons's drift immediately. "It's a plea for help," he agreed.

"Definitely. A cry for assistance. The desperate signal of one of society's victims. Somebody who needs attention." Lyons gave a grim wink and shifted the chunk of cast iron to a more comfortable position.

"So what're you going to do?" repeated Gene-O.

"Give 'em some."

"Some what?"

"Attention."

Father and son thought that over for several moments. Finally Gene gestured at the ugly hunk of iron in Lyons's arms. "What's that for?"

Lyons looked up in mock surprise. "Why, isn't it a search warrant?"

Gene-O was quick on the uptake on this one. "It looks like one to me," he said innocently, a smile spreading over his features. "I've never seen one, of course, but that's exactly what I'd always figured one must look like."

"Looks like one to me," Lyons responded. "That's why I picked it up. I think it's a search warrant. I'm pretty sure it's one, in fact." As an afterthought he added, "I wouldn't be standing here holding it if it wasn't one, would I?"

Gene shook his head. "I wouldn't think so."

"Me, neither," Gene-O agreed. "Is it a good search warrant?" he asked innocently after a few seconds.

"It looks like a good one to me," Lyons said.

"Well, it looks good to me, too," Gene-O said, "but you understand, I don't know a lot about legal things."

Lyons lowered his head and pretended to examine the chunk of rusty scrap iron. "Yep," he announced finally, a smile tugging at the corners of his mouth.

"It's a good one?"

"One of the best."

"Do you know how to work one? A search warrant?"

Lyons shrugged. "I used to. I think I can still figure out this kind, anyway."

"How does it work?"

"Like this. Watch. It's easy."

He turned toward the duplex. The front door to the dilapidated structure was directly in front of him. Then, using the cylinder head both to increase his weight or mass—and therefore momentum—and to protect his body, the Ironman turned and charged toward the closed front door.

2

Two hundred and eighty pounds or thereabouts—say two hundred for the Ironman and eighty or so for the iron—hit the door of the duplex at a hard charge.

It was never any contest, at least after one brief, heart-stopping moment.

Surprisingly the door proved to be more solid than it first appeared. To be sure, it had seen better days—most of the paint was gone, and whatever remained clung to the wood in curled-up patches. But beneath all the neglect lay a different matter entirely.

Moments before, Lyons had sized it up with an appraising eye. He had kicked in his share—and then some—of doors in his time. And when he began his charge at this one, he was confident he could put his fist, shoulder or body right through it, no sweat.

With the cylinder head as lead man, it should be easy. And it was.

Almost.

The instant he struck, Lyons realized that this wasn't the flimsy, run-down, hollow-core affair he had envisioned. Instead, he was up against a real, live, solid wood exterior door, one that wasn't about to give way easily. For the briefest moment he had visions of being stopped—convincingly and embarrassingly—in his tracks in the midst of his charge.

He shouldn't have worried.

As with most matchbox houses like the duplex, the actual door itself was surrounded by a wooden frame. When the house had been built, the frame had been set into the walls and then nailed into place against the vertical studs. Ultimately, when the house had been finished, the exterior stucco had covered the studs and had gone clear up to the edge of the doorframe.

That was when it had been new.

Lyons guessed that the building was at least twenty-five years old. It had seen a lot of heavy wear and tear since that time. Neglect and abuse had combined to weaken the nailing that joined the frame of the door to the studs. Although the door was solid enough, and was held to the frame by the hinges on one side and the lock on the other, the frame itself was the weak link. The results were spectacular.

"Rrrrrgghhh!"

It began as a growl and grew to a roar as Lyons closed the gap at a hard run. Cylinder head leading, man and iron hit the door with a crash.

The entire structure shook from the impact. Far down the walls, several feet from the door, the only two windows that hadn't been broken, rattled noisily in their frames. The screech of reluctant nails being pulled out of dried wood cut through all the other sounds.

The door held.

The frame around it didn't.

Both door and frame tore loose from the ancient studding that supported them. As a single unit, they crashed flat on the floor inside the living room.

Lyons staggered and very nearly went down, his balance disrupted by the initial resistance of the doorframe. Then, cylinder head still gripped ahead of him, he leaped forward to regain his footing. He ended up standing just inside the doorway, poised atop the now-flattened door like a surfer riding the big one.

"Cowabunga! Surf's up!" he roared, recalling the terms that were in vogue when he was a kid surfing off the beaches in L.A.

Beneath his feet, where the floor should be, were the door and frame. Behind him, where the door should be, was nothing more than a hole in the wall.

It was urban renewal, Stony Man style.

Lyons glanced around the room, his eyes taking an instant inventory of the shabby apartment.

Straight ahead lay a dining area and kitchen. Immediately to his right was the living room. On the opposite wall, a door led to a hallway that joined the bedroom and bathroom.

The whole place smelled hot and fetid, despite the occasional shots of cool from the wall-mounted air conditioner that clattered noisily on Gene's electricity.

Ahead, in the dining area, stood a rectangular table. It had metal legs, once shiny but now pitted and rough, and a green Formica surface. Three chairs surrounded it. Two of them looked as if they had originally matched the table, all part of the same cheap dinette set. They were also metal and had matching green plastic-covered pads on their seats. Dingy white stuffing showed through splits in the green plastic, pushing up from the openings like festering wounds.

The third chair was made of wood slats. A huge man, naked to the waist, sat heavily on it, his bulk all but concealing the chair.

He was an immense, hairy beast, fat but hard fat, as Lyons's football coach had once called it. Big frame, heavily muscled, then layered with fat. The heat brought beads of sweat that gathered and formed droplets in the man's thick, matted body hair. His torso gleamed where the hair wasn't so dense. Lurid tattoos—a twisted tangle of snakes—ran down his meaty arms.

A buffalo, Lyons realized, using the slang term popular among outlaw bikers for a big, brutish animal like the one before him.

For a split second Lyons thought the man was in fact an outlaw biker he had once tangled with. Krasne had been the man's name. Crank Krasne.

This guy looked like an older, heavier Crank Krasne, an outlaw biker who had killed because he liked to and just for the hell of it sometimes, a man who had been responsible for the deaths of Mike Chandler and Danny Williams and a slew of other people.

But he couldn't be Krasne, of course, because Lyons had killed Krasne, had hunted him down with Gadgets Schwarz, Politician and Mike Chandler, and had shot him in the chest with a .45 Government Model even as Crank had held a girl as hostage and shield. He'd shot him again and again and again, but the man refused to die until Lyons had put one into his head, and that had ended it for sure.

No, this guy wasn't Crank, but he looked just as dangerous. If you hit him with a baseball bat, Lyons bet it wouldn't faze him, but the bat would vibrate all the way up your arms and then make you vibrate as well.

Lyons's trained eye caught something else as well. An ugly-looking .45 pistol, the standard Colt Government Model by the looks of it, lay on the table.

The gun's blue finish was gone, and the general color of the weapon had become the brown of rust. But, from where Lyons stood, there was nothing to indicate that it was inoperable.

A rusty .45 could still make a hole in you, Lyons knew. And the hole would be just like the one made by a shiny blue

.45, namely, forty-five-hundredths of an inch across where it went in, and maybe twice that where it exited, depending on the ammo and how much it expanded as it tore through the meat of the body.

In the same sweeping glance, Lyons took in the living room.

Most of the room lay off to his right—the door he now stood on had been at the left side of the room. No couch or sofa, no chairs, no TV even. A single king-size mattress without sheets lay on the floor to the far right, directly beneath the air conditioner.

A skinny man with long, greasy brown hair had obviously been screwing a grubby-looking blond woman on the mattress. Her eyes were glazed and unfocused from whatever drugs she had ingested.

As a cop, Lyons had stumbled into more than one scene like this. Usually the only word that described it was "bleak." This time was no exception.

For a long moment the scene stayed frozen.

The buffalo at the table gaped at him in amazement. The man on the bed gazed in shocked disbelief at the blond man standing on top of what had been the door. His eyes focused and then defocused. He turned away and then turned back to see if the vision was still there. Lyons could imagine him wondering what acid trip this was a flashback to, or what weird shit he had gotten in his last dope.

Then things started to happen.

"What the fuck?" snarled the big man by the table as he reached for the .45.

"Freeze!" barked Lyons. "Sex police!"

The buffalo had evidently been on the receiving end of enough police attention in his day to recognize the authority in Lyons's voice, at least until the "sex police" part.

He froze.

At that moment, Gene and Gene-O burst through the door behind Lyons. Gene carried something that looked like the handle from an old pick or ax. Gene-O held a rusty crowbar that he must have picked up in the junk outside.

Gene, incensed at his electric bill, angered by the heat and fired up by Lyons's reckless charge, gestured sharply with the ax handle toward the couple on the mattress. "You!" he snapped. "You're stealing my electricity!"

The man's face contorted uncomprehendingly as his mind attempted to assimilate what was happening to him.

Gene-O was just as quick on the uptake. "Don't they need a license to do that?" he asked as he spotted the couple on the mattress. "They can't do that without a license, can they?"

"Or at least a permit," responded his father. "Gotta have at least a permit."

"Learner's permit," agreed Gene-O. "From the looks of it, a learner's permit would be about their speed."

By this time, the buffalo at the table had realized that Lyons wasn't a cop, though he sure as hell had sounded like one. Moreover, he had also realized that none of the men had firearms.

With a snarl of anger he reached again for the .45.

Lyons hurled the cylinder head at him.

The Ironman had been holding the chunk of steel at approximately chest level. He simply thrust both arms out and up at an angle, pushing the cylinder head in an arc toward the fat man, like a basketball push-pass from the chest.

It landed in the man's lap an instant before his hand closed on the pistol.

With a crash the chair collapsed, shattered by the eighty-odd pounds so suddenly added to the buffalo's already heavy frame. The grasping hand caught only empty air.

"Fuckerrr!"

The man roared the oath as his bulk hit the floor. Lyons didn't hesitate. He bounded ahead and grabbed the .45 from the table before the buffalo could struggle free of the debris from the chair and the chunk of engine.

Deftly Lyons checked the pistol. Rusty, sure. But the clip was full of silver-tips. There was one in the chamber, and the pistol was cocked with the safety on. "Cocked and locked," they called it.

A flick of the thumb meant it would be ready for business.

Dancing back out of range of the big man, Lyons turned to the other two people in the room.

Neither of them had moved. Gene and Gene-O still stood, ready for trouble, makeshift clubs in hand.

Suddenly this had become fun, Lyons realized. He had been moping around, in a sense, for weeks, feeling unhappy but not really knowing why. It was as if he were overwhelmed by the futility of it all—what did laying his ass on the line ever accomplish?

This was different. Here he was acting crazy, taking a chance for no reason other than because he wanted to, to help his friends. It wasn't a mission; it was a lark. And he was enjoying the hell out of it.

He decided to carry on in the same vein begun by Gene and his son.

"Well?" he roared. "You heard him, asshole! You got a license?"

The skinny man gulped, his Adam's apple bobbing up and down. Still he remained silent.

Taking a step forward, Lyons continued. "You gotta have a license, man! A permit! A license to fuck! No license, I gotta arrest you for violating 12500 of the Vehicle Code. You read me, pal?"

Still half dazed, the man nodded uncomprehendingly. Lyons walked over until he was standing directly in front of the naked couple. Then he bent down and put his face a few inches from the skinny's man face.

"Well, let's see it! Let's see that license, pal!" After that they handled the energy theft with a certain finality.

The air conditioner was ripped out of the wall, courtesy of Gene-O's crowbar. Gene gathered up the heavy orange extension cord and followed it outside and back to his gym to unplug it. While he was there, he got a pair of diagonal cutters, or "dikes." Then he dumped the extension cord on the floor next to the green table, near the buffalo who still sat with the cylinder head on his lap.

Using the dikes, Gene cut the extension cord into six- or eight-inch lengths.

It took a while because it was a long cord, probably twenty or thirty feet, which meant fifty-odd little lengths of extension cord.

Lyons also did a cursory search of the house, for safety's sake as much as anything else. In the course of that search, he found four ounces of dope—methamphetamine powder or "crank" in a plastic bag. They also found eleven hundred dollars in cash.

"You!" Lyons barked at the buffalo.

The man didn't answer, but just glared at him.

"You wouldn't be dealing this stuff now, would you?" he demanded. "Supplying it to the neighborhood kids, maybe?"

The man still didn't answer.

Lyons tried again. "Is this your dope?"

The buffalo glowered at him. Lyons shrugged and repeated his question to the skinny man on the mattress. No answer there, either.

"I guess it don't belong to anybody," the Ironman said at last. "Poor, unloved meth. Nobody wants you."

He strode out over the flattened door until he was outside the house. Then, turning so the buffalo could see him, he emptied the bag into the weeds, waving it in the air to scatter the powder across the dirt.

The hatred on the buffalo's face was almost tangible as Lyons walked back into the house. He picked up the money and counted just enough to pay for Gene's electric bill, then he took the gun from Gene-O.

"You two guys wait outside," he said.

Father and son looked at him, hesitated, then shrugged and left. Lyons knelt down next to the buffalo.

"Listen to me, buffalo-breath. Listen real good." Lyons's voice had become soft. Deadly soft. "I know what you're thinking. But don't."

He paused, then continued. "Don't think it. Any of it. Don't think about coming after me. Don't think about coming after my friends, or going next door and burning their gym, or anything like that."

The big man's eyes stared at the gun in Lyons's hand. The Ironman continued.

"You've just become an insurance company. That's right. You're now just like a piece of the rock, a real, live insurance company. You know what I mean, pal?"

The buffalo didn't answer, but his eyes flicked up to meet Lyons's.

"Why, if anything bad happens to them, anything at all, I'm gonna assume you did it. And I'm gonna take it out of your ass, one piece at a time. See? Anything happens to them, and you pay up."

Lyons's face had twisted into an icy smile. It was a smile in name only, due to the shape of his mouth, but it held no warmth or humor whatsoever.

"If they get mugged, I'll know you're behind it. If their gym catches fire, I'll know you're behind it. If a fucking meteor falls out of the fucking sky and turns their place into a crater, I'll know you were behind that, too."

The cold smile vanished. Lyons's eyes narrowed.

"And I'll collect on the policy. I'll come after you. I'll find you. And I'll kill you."

Lyons reached forward and patted the buffalo on the cheek. It wasn't a very hard pat, not a slap, but it wasn't exactly friendly, either.

"Do yourself a favor. Believe this like you've never believed anything in your life."

He got to his feet and unloaded the .45, then tossed the empty weapon to the floor. When he reached the gaping doorway, Lyons turned and smiled.

"Welcome to the insurance business."

He turned and walked out into the heat.

Afterward, they all agreed it had been a pretty stupid performance. And yet, it was precisely the sort of foolhardy stunt that legends are made of among fighting men everywhere. It made for an outlook, a sort of reckless courage, essential to the personality a man has to have to risk his life for people he doesn't even know.

Gene had it. Lyons had it. And even Gene-O had courage, though he had never been in the military or in a line of work that called for it.

When you jump out of an airplane at night over enemy territory, and rely on your chute to save you until you hit the ground, and your guts after that, you tend to be a little reckless in other things as well. Gene had done that, as had Lyons's Able Team partner Rosario "Politician" Blancanales, each of whom had once been members of the Special Forces.

When you're poised outside a door, gun in hand, ready to go in fast, knowing the bad guys are inside and are watching the door, waiting to blow your guts out, it changes your outlook on life. Lyons had done that more times than he could count.

For some reason he didn't worry about saturated fat or his cholesterol level. He should be so lucky to live long enough for it to be a problem.

3

They took the house easy, no sweat.

Actually it wasn't even L.A. that they finally hit; it was Encino in the San Fernando Valley, home of the malls and birthplace—or spawning ground—of the valley girls.

Like, grodie to the max and gag me with a spoon.

Like, you go to the Galleria, you know? It's that really monster mall, right next to 101, before you get to Ventura Boulevard. And then you go, like, over that way—I'm not good at directions, you know—and it's kind of up there, like towards Chatsworth but not really, you know...

They located the place on Monday. They took it down on Tuesday. And, as with their usual MO, they were in another state by Wednesday.

G.M. and Slimy had done the recon work to select the house.

Even that aspect sometimes posed a problem, because unlike the actual raid, it had to be done in the daytime. That meant being visible to the people who lived in whatever neighborhoods they happened to be checking out.

The problem was that anybody who saw them was likely to remember them. If the person were nervous, he might just call the cops to check them on g.p.—general principle—given the way they looked. And any cop who saw them would jump at the chance to stop them for a friendly little chat.

Recon fell to Slimy and G.M. sort of by default.

G.M., at six-four and two-forty or so, wasn't exactly inconspicuous. But Eight Ball, big as a buffalo, with his deadfish white skin, the shocking skull tattoos and the digit on his cranium, was out of the question. Hell, anybody who even got a glimpse of him would remember him forever. And Whip wasn't any better—the eyes on that lean psycho bastard made him as unforgettable as his monster companion.

And Slimy—he looked okay, but he was too stupid to do the recon himself. So G.M. had rented a T-bird, and he and Slimy had gone out driving in Encino in the heart of the San Fernando Valley. Slimy drove and G.M. looked.

They knew generally what they were looking for. And G.M. also knew he would recognize it when they found it. As one of the Supreme Court justices had said in a case on hard-core obscenity, it's hard to define, but you know it when you see it.

In general terms, they were looking for a damn nice house in a damn nice neighborhood. A big house on a big lot, say a half acre or better. The kind of house that went for, say, a quarter mil a crack.

A house that was set back from the street—for privacy.

A house that maybe had some trees and vegetation or a wall between it and the street—again for privacy.

A house close to the freeway, or close to main arteries that were close to freeways.

Surprisingly, though, what they were *not* looking for were the homes of the ultrarich, the super mansions lived in by the big movie stars, recording artists and Arab sheikhs, the Beverly Hills or Laurel Canyon places.

G.M. shook his head in disgust. That was another reason they couldn't send Slimy out alone to do the recon work, he thought. Dumb bastard would have found some palace for them to try to take out.

"Why can't we take down one of them real ritzy places?" Slimy had once inquired.

That had been in another city, not L.A., on one of their earlier capers. They had been sitting in a motel room, going through tourist literature and trying to figure out where to begin the reconnaissance.

"Huh?" G.M. had been studying a map and hadn't heard him initially.

Slimy had repeated his question.

G.M. had given him a disgusted look, but hadn't replied. But the idea had appealed to Whip, aka Psycho, and he'd taken up the thread.

"Slimy's right, G.M. Why can't we take off one of them really fancy joints? The super, super rich bastards will never know what hit 'em."

"Probably be more shit to steal inside that, too," chimed in Slimy.

G.M. put his map aside and gazed at his two companions grimly. Finally he shook his head, his annoyance clearly visible. When he spoke, his voice was rude, almost taunting.

"A real fancy joint, huh?"

"Yeah, that's right, G.M. Some place like that." Slimy nodded eagerly as he spoke.

"Big fucking place with big walls all around it and a gate and servants that greet you at your car? Place like that?"

"Just like that," agreed Slimy.

"Place where they probably wear diamonds and furs to the goddamn shitter? That kinda place?"

By then Slimy had evidently realized G.M. wasn't seriously asking the questions. If he had possessed more than a fifth-grade education, he might have recognized them as rhetorical questions, asked to make a point rather than to really get an answer.

Perhaps he even sensed the big man's impending anger. In any event, this time he didn't respond.

G.M. went on, a venomous edge to his voice.

"Because, shit-for-brains, because places like that got something else, too. And you know what that is?"

Again Slimy didn't respond.

G.M. turned to Whip. "How 'bout you, Psycho? You know what those kinda places got? Something that we don't need?"

Their lean companion also evidently felt it would be wise to remain mute.

"Try guards," spat G.M., belching as he spoke.

"I ain't afraida no guards," muttered Whip. "Just like I ain't afraida cops, neither."

G.M.'s eyes narrowed dangerously. "Places like that, they're likely to be crawling with goddamn guards. And they have alarm systems that make Fort Knox look like shit. And they got direct lines to the police and the sheriff and probably the fucking National Guard, too, 'cause those rich bastards are all in bed together."

Determined to make one last try, to save face if nothing else, Slimy ventured again, "We can handle guards and cops, can't we, G.M.?"

When the big man replied, his voice had lost the taunt. He spoke condescendingly, the way a concerned parent would to a six-year-old child.

"Sure we can, guys. It's just that most of them places are way up away from the freeways. Up real windy roads and shit. And we'll have to fight our way past guards, and then the cops will be all over our ass with SWAT and helicopters. And people who live in places like that, they all have big fucking safes where they keep the valuable shit anyway.

We'd better stick to other types of places, the kind where ordinary big-shot executives live. Fancy, but not too fancy. They got most of the goodies, but less of the drawbacks.''

That had become their MO. It worked, and they had stuck with it.

By Monday evening they had found the perfect place.

Hollings Avenue, just off Ventura Boulevard, not too far from a couple of freeways. The house was a sprawling, California ranch style home made of adobelike stucco, set well back from the street on a three-quarter-acre lot. It had a red tile roof and a three-car garage.

And it was built for privacy.

Between the front entrance and the street ran a five-foot-high stucco wall. Along the wall grew tangled bougainvillea bushes some fifteen feet high. The lawn area was on the outside of all this, leading down to the street.

Cruising by in the rented T-bird, G.M. knew he had found what they were looking for.

"Go up to the end of the street and make a U-turn," he directed.

Slimy complied. As they returned, G.M. checked it out again.

Damn good, he thought. No, hell, it was perfect. From the street only the tops of the windows, the red tile roof behind the privacy wall and the tangle of burgundy-flowered bougainvillea were visible. A Mercedes station wagon was parked in the drive.

And, as they drove slowly past, the garage door began to open. A blond woman in her middle or late thirties came out and walked toward the Mercedes. She wore a short tennis dress, and she was pretty, her legs trim and tanned, her body tight and youthful. G.M. also got a glimpse of another car, this one a sleek Jaguar sedan, inside the garage.

The woman fumbled in her purse for keys, and at that point G.M. lost sight of her as their car rounded a gentle bend in the street, back in the direction from which they had come.

"That's it," said the marauder. "That's fucking it, for sure."

"That's our target?" inquired Slimy as he stopped at the stop sign and carefully checked traffic in both directions. "The place with the blond babe?"

His passenger nodded grimly.

"Bitchin'!" Slimy was exultant. "We finally got a place to do. It's hit-and-run time, baby, that's for sure."

G.M. didn't respond. He was lost in a silent, seething hatred, borne of the memories of his childhood.

The blond bitch was an added dividend, he thought.

Usually he ran the hit-and-run missions with military precision and an iron fist. Wear camouflage gear even though they wouldn't be hiding in any foliage, the idea being that most witnesses remember only the most distinguishing features of their assailants, and the shock of camou garb somehow served to overwhelm any other perception.

Put camou paint on their faces for the same reason. Give them heavy firepower—M-16s and .45 Government Model autopistols.

Rent a real nice truck, say a flatbed with a clean new box on the back; anything too run down would stand out in that kind of neighborhood. The rental, of course, would be under a false name, using cash. Slimy, being the most normal-looking, would handle that part.

Do it at night, a weeknight, preferably a Monday or Tuesday. After nine was best—people were still up, so a little extra noise wasn't likely to attract official attention, yet it was late enough that phone calls and visitors to the "target" house were unlikely.

Take the place down.

That was always the best part: sneaking up, surrounding it, cutting the phone lines unless they were underground, in which case it became a calculated risk that nobody would be on the phone when you made entry.

Knock on the door.

When it was answered, go in hard and fast. Rap whoever it was on the skull with a .45, just for fun and to show you meant business. Then a fast once-over of the house, dragging the terrified residents out of bed, hauling them out of the shower, throwing them all in a pile in the living room.

Move the truck into the garage. Shut the garage door.

Cart out the loot. Then, if there was any time left over, get friendly with the residents—at least the good-looking female ones.

Secure the petrified people. Then haul ass.

Hit. And then run.

Usually it would be the next morning when the crime was discovered—often midmorning when school or work authorities checked on absentees. By then the truck would have been returned—left at the rental yard, cleaned, prints wiped off, full of gas, with a ten-dollar tip for the attendant who checked it in.

The marauders would be long gone by that time, the loot transferred to their own vehicles or stored in a rented storage locker for later retrieval.

Practice made perfect. And a few simple precautions greatly reduced the chances of getting caught, the most important being, never, but never, fence the stuff in the same county, and preferably not the same state, as it was stolen from.

But this time, thought G.M., this time would be special. The blonde would see to that.

A swarm of images appeared in his mind.

Sara, that bitch.

She was sixteen, going on thirty; he had been just two days past his own sixteenth birthday. Sara, teasing him and leading him on. He was an awkward, gangly teenager then, not yet filled out despite his size. And Sara, with her big tits and tight ass, who entertained a slew of older boyfriends in the back seats of station wagons at the drive-in and on blankets in the hills.

Sara, who taunted him and drove him mad with lust and shame.

He remembered vividly the time she'd pulled down the top of her swimsuit and shown him her breasts. They'd been at the lake, and she'd actually done that, yes, shown him her breasts and asked him if he'd wanted to do "it" with her.

And the miserable youth had stammered and gulped, afraid of trying, ashamed of his lust, driven by the girl's brazen taunts, tormented by the iron-hard lump in his shorts.

And his mother's voice, ringing in his ears, "Rupert, if you get a girl pregnant, I'll kill you!"

"Whazza matter, Rupee? Don't ya wanna do it? You're not afraid of doing *it*, are you? You're not *queer*, are you, Rupee?"

Sara's taunts and his own lust had won, at least in the short run. Face burning, he had said he would like to do "it." They had found a toolshed, a dark green metal affair that was hot and dusty, and there in the suffocating heat amid the sacks of seed and fertilizer they had tried "it," the shy, gangly youth and the experienced Sara. And he had failed. Sara had sneered at him, calling him a fine excuse for a man, and had flounced away, leaving him there in the heat and his humiliation....

With a start, G.M. realized that he wouldn't recognize the blond woman he had seen coming out of the house even if he were to meet her on the street later that same day. He had no recollection whatsoever of the face. All he had seen was Sara—Sara's face instead of the woman's own face, and the woman's trim, tight legs becoming Sara's saucy ass.

He also realized that Slimy was talking to him.

"You okay, boss? Something wrong?"

"Huh? Oh, yeah, I'm okay. What were you sayin'?"

"You looked kinda funny for a minute."

"Skip it. I'm fucking okay, I told you." G.M.'s voice cut like a whip, and his small piglike eyes blazed dangerously.

"All right, all right, man. Just checkin', that's all."

"So don't check. Just drop it."

"Okay, G.M. Whatever you say, man." After a pause, Slimy ventured again. "We gonna do that house for sure, boss? The one with the blonde comin' out of it?"

The bearded giant's eyes gazed unfocused, as though looking back across the void of time.

"Yeah," he said softly. "We're gonna do that one for sure."

4

Old habits die hard, she thought.

Jane Odom shook her head quickly, as though anticipating the beads of perspiration she would shake off during the tennis game. But that would be later. She wasn't playing yet, and she wasn't perspiring. Most of all, it wasn't sweat that she was trying to dislodge.

Feelings.

That's what it was. Feelings. The vague, uneasy feeling that something was wrong. And something else, something that reminded her of someone she refused to allow herself to think about.

She stood in the driveway of her Hollings Avenue home and fumbled in her purse for the keys to the Mercedes. Then she found them. As she took them out, she dropped them on the cement driveway.

"Oh, dammit," she swore softly under her breath as she stooped to pick them up.

What was it that made her feel so nervous? So queasy, almost?

Something about the car that had just gone by, the Thunderbird. Yes, that was it—the car. But what about it?

Think, woman. *Think!* What made you feel that way? What did you see that you don't realize you saw? Replay the tapes in your mind—your mind's video camera. Relax, don't be uptight, just replay the scene. What's there? What are you seeing?

A blue car, new, a passenger sedan. It's sleek and dark blue, almost black.

All right, lady, that's good, said a voice in her mind. It was a gentle, patient sort of voice, and it continued. What kind of car is it?

A Thunderbird, I think. Yes, that's it, a T-bird. Two doors, or did all T-birds have only two doors? Jane didn't know; all she knew was that this one had two and not four.

License plate—hell, you want miracles? Not the number, lady, but the state. Was it California? Or was it an out-of-state plate?

California. A local plate.

Two men inside. No, make that *at least* two men inside. She had seen two, but she couldn't say for sure that that was all there were.

A chill ran down her spine, and she shivered involuntarily. She was definitely on the right track; it was the T-bird that had caused her to have these weird feelings.

She went on, replaying the tapes, the voice in her mind asking herself gentle questions, no pressure, never prodding, just calling her attention to things.

One of the men had a beard. The passenger. He was big, huge even. She could tell that even with him sitting down in the car. That meant he had to be really big. Then she remembered that the window had been rolled down, and the passenger had had his elbow sticking out, the underside of the arm resting on the doorframe.

What was it about that? Oh, yeah, the guy's arm was big. It had thick, big muscles. Not fat, just big, like a powerlifter's arm. So the guy was big, huge, and he was a weight lifter type.

What were they wearing, lady?

She thought, then shook her head. Sorry, can't help you with that one.

All right. So what was it about them that seems funny to you?

I don't know, she answered herself. They just seemed strange, that's all. As if they meant trouble. As if they were thinking bad thoughts. I know it isn't much to go on, but that's how I felt after they drove by. Oh, yes, they drove slowly, too, as if they were looking for something.

The little voice in her mind replied to that one. Nothing illegal about that. Maybe they were just looking for a friend's house? Did it seem like that?

No, it didn't. Like I said, they just gave off bad vibes. I know it sounds silly, but...

Suddenly the weird feelings were there again, and this time they weren't related just to the big men in the car. They came from something else, too, something that had to do with the big man, but something more.

Then she had it.

Her ex-husband. The whole thing reminded her of her ex-husband. The cop.

But that was another lifetime. She never thought about him—correction, she never let herself think about him. And when she did, the feelings returned, and she would have to deal with them.

She handled it differently these days. Not the way she once had.

In the past she would have to wrench her mind away from him, literally tear it away. She would do that and take him and throw him and all the memories into a big room in her mind and slam and lock the door and lean against the door with all her strength to keep the memories where they belonged, locked away in the past.

It hurts too much if they come out where you can see them.

Now she handled it another way, one that didn't require such iron control of her emotions, one that allowed herself to feel and then get over it.

She didn't try to fight them any longer; she let the memories wash over her and recede. It was like a big wave in the ocean, the kind when you're at the beach and the tide is coming in. Three or four waves come along that are just normal, and then the next one comes high and covers over the words you had scraped in the sand, so that when it washes back there's nothing but a few trace marks left.

In her case it was a wave of feeling. It built up, surged over her and then finally retreated, as that part of her life became another few minutes farther in the past.

He had been a cop. And, in the part of her life when they had been together, she had shared the cop's life with him.

He had been a good cop. Fair. Tough or gentle, or both, depending on what he had going at the time.

It was *his* voice in her mind, asking the questions, gently prodding, pointing, helping her to "look over here," and "look over there."

It was through him that she knew what a powerlifter's arm looked like. It was through him that she knew witnesses often saw more than they remembered, and that if you were a gentle, patient questioner, you could often get them to look at it again and see more. It was almost like hypnosis in a way, only different.

The wave washed up over her, over the words and dreams scraped into the beach sand.

Where was he today? What was he doing? Did he remember the years together the way she did, with the same sweet, sad fondness? It would never be again, it *could* never be again, but that didn't change one thing.

They had been good years. And while they were good, those good times had been her reality. So that part of her life—at least until the last couple of years—had been a good life.

A life is what you experience as you go along, not where you are when you end up, she thought. Hell, even that was one of *his* sayings. But it was true.

Jane was entitled to remember those years that way. And she would remember them that way.

But one more thing was certain, too. The past was, indeed, the past. History. There were cars on the road that hadn't been thought of when they'd been married. There were new products, and new ways to package old products, a host of things to reinforce that this was today's world, and yesterday's had passed.

The wave started to recede. Every minute, every hour, every day, those things became farther in the past. *Now* was what counted. She lived in the now, the present, today and tomorrow.

And the present was good, too. Different, but good. In many ways better, certainly better than what the other had become when it was finally pronounced dead.

The present wasn't cops and witnesses and death and courts. She wasn't Janie Lyons anymore. Today she was Janie Odom, and her husband was Steve Odom, vice president of SanDor Corporation, a high-tech computer company.

Janie and Steve. Steve and Janie.

They made a good couple, people said. Steve was tall and rangy, almost a foot taller than she. He was kind and caring and competent, and he took care of her and mended that part of her that she thought would never recover—her heart. They had two kids of their own, in addition to Tommy, and

Steve made a lot of money. Most of all, though, she knew he would never leave her.

She glanced at her watch. She was late for tennis.

Maybe it wasn't really anything about the T-bird, she rationalized. Maybe it was just all part of thinking about the past, triggered by some unknown stimulus.

Still, the bearded guy had given off bad vibes. If she saw that car in the neighborhood again, cruising slowly like that, she'd call the police.

Behind the wheel of the Mercedes, she wondered what Carl was doing these days. But she only thought about it for a moment.

5

At eight minutes after nine that Tuesday evening, the doorbell at the Odoms' house rang.

Jane frowned and glanced at her husband. He was hunched over a pile of papers on the kitchen table. He shrugged and gestured at the papers, a wordless request that she answer the door.

"Who could it be this late?" she asked, more to herself than to her husband. "You expecting anybody?"

He shook his head. "The kids?" he suggested.

"Maybe. I'd have thought we'd get a call first, though, if something was wrong."

Still, as she thought it over, that had to be it. Must be something to do with the kids. All three of them were away for the evening—a sleep-over at the Johnstons. Steve was going out of town on business the next day and had to look over the papers first. Just an hour, he had promised her.

Maybe one of them had forgotten something, a toy, perhaps for the littlest one, something she couldn't sleep without. And in that case, it would be Bruce at the door, asking for whatever had been forgotten. Jane pulled her robe more tightly around her and answered the door.

Later, the authorities would put the time at nine minutes after nine.

A lean, muscular man stood outside the door.

He was dressed like a wild man, with brown and black and green paint all over his face. He grabbed her by the forearm, yanked her toward him and forced his way inside all in one motion.

"Steve!" she cried out. "Steve, look—"

The wild man smacked her on the side of the face with the gun he held in his hand.

The blow snapped her head sideways and made her eyes swim. For an instant Jane thought she would lose consciousness. Then she steadied herself and regained control.

At that instant she felt—she *knew*—the bearded man in the Thunderbird yesterday was behind this. She couldn't see him, and he certainly wasn't the one at the door, but he was involved. She knew it.

Suddenly her eyes went blurry, and Jane knew she had been wrong about how hard the lean man had hit her. She felt her knees buckle and realized she was going to pass out.

Jane was vaguely conscious of the lean man hauling her, wrenching her to one side in the entrance hallway to the house—her house—then dropping her. As she fell, the fact that she was only wearing her nightgown beneath the robe flashed through her mind. Then her head hit the tile of the entryway, and she was out.

An indeterminate time later, she became aware of things around her once again.

It was a slow process, however. First, she felt something rough but soft beneath her face, and then beneath her arms, her breasts, her stomach and her legs. Then she became aware of the color, a light brown, and realized that she was lying on the living room carpet.

Rough but soft.

Her mind did crazy things. Can something be both rough and soft at the same time? Maybe. The texture was rough, the padding soft.

What a thing to be thinking about, part of her mind said.

Then she became aware of activity going on around her. People lifting things, unplugging the stereo and the TV and the VCR, taking things out into the garage through the doorway off the kitchen.

It must be moving day, she thought. Yes, that's it. They were moving. The movers were there, carrying things out.

But where were they moving?

Jane frowned to herself. She didn't remember deciding to move. She certainly didn't remember packing. Well, maybe Steve had taken care of all that. Yes, that must be it. Steve had had the packing people in while she was playing tennis yesterday.

Something about going to tennis stirred her memory. She couldn't quite remember what it was, but it had something to do with a Thunderbird. It wasn't a good feeling, though, not a pleasant thing to think about. A man was involved with the moving, too, in some way she couldn't exactly pinpoint. Perhaps he was helping them move.

Steve could take care of all that. He always took care of things like that.

She really didn't want to move. Then she changed her position to get more comfortable.

Again she felt the roughness of the carpet against her skin. Then she realized that her robe was missing, that she was naked.

She frowned. That didn't seem right. Maybe she should get dressed, put something else on. But the men didn't seem to mind. In fact, nobody seemed to be paying much attention to her at all.

Still, Steve wouldn't like it, her being undressed like that. She would ask Steve to bring her a robe.

Where was Steve, anyway? Was all this a dream? A bad dream about moving, about being taken away from her security, the things she knew and liked?

She pushed herself up off the carpet and looked around, putting her right forearm against her body, across her breasts, at the same time.

"Steve?" she called. "Steve, can you get me a robe? Steve, honey, where are you?"

A sudden movement to her left, just barely within her peripheral vision, caused her to jerk her head that way. A sickening, nauseating pain washed over her. It radiated from the side of her head where the man had hit her with the gun, and she staggered from its force. As if through the haze, she realized it was one of the movers who had moved.

Except that he wasn't a mover at all; he was a soldier of some kind.

The man was average size, a white guy, with dark hair. He wore camouflage clothing, soldier fatigues. He had painted his face the same mottled green/brown/black as the man at the door. He had some stubby sort of machine gun in his hands. It was a blunt, ugly thing, a flat green color.

The movement Jane had seen had been caused by his leaping to one side and bringing the gun to bear on her at the same time.

Suddenly Jane realized she recognized him. He had been the driver of the Thunderbird. Not the big guy, not the huge man with the beard, but the other one.

At the same time, she felt something tickling the side of her face. It must be perspiration, she thought.

Angrily she wiped it away. She used her left forearm, keeping the right one clamped to her breasts. She reached around and wiped the trickle of sweat off the right side of her face.

A smear of bright red covered her arm.

"You're not movers!" she shrieked.

The man looked at her in amazement.

"Where's Steve?" she screamed. "What have you done with my husband?"

The man took a quick step forward and slapped her hard. The force of the blow spun her around, and she fell half across the couch, catching herself with her left hand. For a moment she thought she would be sick. She clamped her throat against the waves of nausea that washed over her.

Somebody else moved in the room.

Jane looked up and saw the bearded man. He was dressed like the lean one at the door and the driver of the T-bird.

Jane looked again. Yes, it was the bearded man. No amount of camouflage paint could hide that.

So the vibes had been right after all.

Jane screamed.

She wheeled around to flee and screamed again as she ran into a fourth man. He was gigantic, not muscular like the bearded man, but massive, like a mastodon, all huge bones and solid, unyielding meat. He, too, wore camou paint on his face, but his arms and the top of his head were bare, and he hadn't put paint on them.

The man's skin was a deathly white, the stark white of marble and corpses.

A chain of skulls, tattoos, ran up each arm and disappeared beneath the sleeveless camouflage vest that he wore. There was something dark on the top of the man's head; she caught a glimpse of it, but couldn't be sure what it was.

The man grinned at her, a hideous visage of missing teeth in an evil, hairless face. A deep gash ran across his forehead. Blood had mixed and diluted and smeared the camouflage paint. It had coagulated; she could see the little crimson jellylike lumps in the furrow of the wound.

Jane screamed, and screamed, and screamed again. Then she saw Steve.

Her husband lay on the floor, near the wall of the living room. He lay at a funny angle, or angles, sprawled almost as if he didn't have bones in his body. One arm was askew, the other underneath him. The carpet near his mouth was stained dark red.

"Steve!" she screamed. Then, her voice breaking, she sobbed the name again and again. "Oh, Steve, Steve."

The bearded man spoke to her. His voice rumbled from his chest, and she knew she was hearing the voice of evil, pure, unadulterated, one hundred percent evil.

"Sara!"

Jane whirled around to face the bearded man, evidently the leader. Who was Sara?

"What'za matter, Sara?"

Jane looked carefully at the man. His eyes burned brightly, and his face looked animated, hyper. And then she realized that he thought she was Sara.

"Sorry about your new boyfriend, Sara. But the dumb bastard hit my friend Eight Ball, and we had to kill him a little."

Jane glanced back at the livid wound on the mastodon's forehead. Then she saw the fireplace poker. It was on the floor, near the kitchen. It was bent double, and she saw the smears of red on one end of it.

She could deduce what happened.

Steve, her sweet, brave, loving Steve, had grabbed the first weapon handy—the fireplace poker. Then he must have let the big man have it with the stout metal rod. And, tall and rangy though he was, Steve was strong. Judging from the gash on the mastodon's skull, it had been a hell of a good shot, too.

And then they had, they had . . . what had they done to him? "Killed him a little." What did that mean?

Was he dead?

The bearded leader was speaking again, his voice sounding as if it came from the pit of hell. "Not so funny now, Sara, is it? Not like before, right, Sara?"

Still keeping one arm across her breasts, Jane looked closely at the big man, trying to figure out what was going on with him.

"You laughed at me, Sara. You teased me. You . . ."

He said something else, but Janie no longer heard him. A strange sort of calm had come over her.

It had started when she'd looked at the fireplace poker and seen the blood on the business end of it. Business end— that was a funny phrase. The business end of a shovel, knife, spear. The part that did the work, did the business.

Who used that term? Where had she gotten it from?

No matter. Her mind was working, sifting, shifting. She was clicking into the survival mode.

Steve was either dead or he wasn't. She couldn't change that now. And either way he couldn't help her. It was up to her.

Thank God the kids weren't there.

That's all you've got, lady, she told herself. When the chips are down, the only one you can completely rely on is you. No matter how tough it gets, it comes down to you. Others can help—help a lot sometimes—but in the end, you are your final fallback, your last option.

Who had told her that?

When you look death in the face, that's who you've got. You. Nobody else but yourself. You and the universe, you and your life, you and your death.

You can give up. That's the easy way, maybe. It probably won't hurt too much, and it might even be quick.

Or you can fight.

One way you lose. The other way you stand a chance. Or even end up with a draw, which would be better than losing but not as good as winning. And you have to do something. Either way it's your decision.

It's up to you.

Fight. Just go mad-dog, psycho, like a wildcat on PCP. Or let yourself be led to the slaughterhouse like a steer.

She looked at the big man with the beard and laughed, laughed out loud, laughed in his face.

His face froze, then contorted with anger. "You bitch!" he bellowed.

But she had already turned away toward the mastodon with the horrible gash in his head.

"Please," she whispered, her voice pleading. "Please help me. Please."

The mastodon stood, uncertain, as if unable to resolve the conflict between the woman's pleading and the bearded man's rage. Jane took a quick step forward and kneed him solidly in the groin, a satisfying, hard shot that carried all the force of her body behind it. Then she dodged quickly around him and sprinted toward the rear of the house.

Behind her, she could hear the whistling grunt as the mastodon curled himself around his damaged privates. She also heard the roar of the bearded man.

"Get her!"

Jane dashed around the corner and into the long hall that led to the back of the house. Straight ahead was the back bedroom, which had a bed and dresser in it, but which they used for guests.

She didn't hesitate an instant.

Still sprinting, Jane leaped onto the bed and dived head-first out the plate-glass window into the darkness that separated her house from the neighbor's. She hit and hurt herself, but it didn't hurt, not really. Then she was on her feet and running into the night.

6

Lyons put some fresh flowers on the grave and then went to meet Blancanales and Schwarz at the airport.

He wondered if the flowers served any purpose for anybody besides himself. Specifically he wondered if she knew—wherever she was—that he was putting them there.

The cemetery was vast and neat. It had rolling hills and marked roadways and was divided into quadrants or sectors to help locate specific gravesites. Part of it, the older part, located clear on the opposite side of the cemetery from her grave, had upright markers and monuments. But where Margaret was buried there weren't any. Instead, her grave was identified by a neat, flat rectangular slab of marble that could be mowed over.

Her name, Margaret Elaine Williams, was carved into the marble in neat, precise letters. The lines of the letters tapered down to a point, like little trenches with a V-shape cross section, the point at the bottom.

Lyons wondered what it would be like to be the guy whose job was to make those carvings. What did he, whoever he was, think of? Did he wonder who the names had belonged to? What those persons had done in their lives? How they had died, and who had been left behind when they had?

What the hell, he thought suddenly. It's probably all done by machine now, anyway.

Beneath Margaret's name was the birthdate and the date of death. As always, Lyons did the subtraction in his head. The difference was thirty-two years.

It seemed kind of short somehow.

Beneath the dates were two lines in Latin, a total of seven words etched into the marble.

> Terra es, Terram ibis
> Requiescat in Pace

The second one, *Requiescat in Pace*, Lyons knew. Rest in Peace, the RIP of countless movies, cartoons and other, real graves. The pragmatic part of him wondered if the abbreviation had come about because of the cost of marble and the difficulty of hand-carving it.

The first line wasn't so common. It had been contained in a handwritten letter Margaret had left behind, to be opened on her death. She had apparently written it shortly before her last trip with Lyons, the one in which they had quarreled and then parted.

The letter had been in part a will, leaving most of her property to a sister who lived back east somewhere. But it had been more than that. It had also contained three pages of her thoughts on life and death. In the letter itself she had referred to that part as a "discourse on the human condition."

She had always been a smart lady, he thought. But pretty much down to earth in other respects.

The Latin phrase had been written in her neat penmanship right after the body of the letter. It had been written just above her name, where "love" or "sincerely" or "see ya" is usually written.

Terra es, Terram ibis.

Lyons hadn't known what the phrase meant, and it had bugged him. He had copied it down and carried it around in his pocket for a week. Finally he had decided to do a little detective work on it. He had looked up the location of the nearest junior college and found a language professor who was able to give him the translation.

Dust thou art, to dust thou returnest.

Lyons often wondered why she had written it, any of it.

She must have done it a week or ten days before she had died, he thought, calculating the dates in light of the events that had unfolded. What had moved her to make a will? Why had she chosen that particular time to set down her thoughts of life—and death—onto paper?

Had she somehow known, or sensed, even subconsciously, what had lain so closely ahead of her?

The Ironman didn't know much Latin, but that was one phrase he would never forget.

Maybe he'd add it to his own epitaph, which would read, "Do it scared if you have to, but fucking do it. If it's right to do, just nut up and do it."

Terra es, Terram ibis tacked onto the end of that just might add a touch of class to his epitaph. Or a touch of fucking class, as Gadgets Schwarz had quipped when Lyons had mentioned it one time when he'd been half sloshed on beer and kamikazes.

Lyons thought of the woman whose remains lay a fathom below where he stood.

She had been "Margie" to him. Years ago he had loved her. Barely twenty-one, he had joined the LAPD. She had been in school, studying psychology. But ultimately it hadn't worked out, and she had gone her way and he had gone his.

His way was to become a superstar young cop. Her way was to become a clinical psychologist, a professional in a profession that was generally critical of police work.

A few years later Lyons met Jane Mahoney. They fell in love and married. Eight years later they were divorced. The final decree of divorce, a single sheet of paper with typing in the preprinted boxes, had cited "irreconcilable differences." The lawyer had said that those were the legal buzzwords to get a divorce.

Irreconcilable differences.

It was like an epitaph, in a way, a single line cut into marble to sum up what had been six pretty good years finally put to rest after a couple of bad ones.

Lyons wondered briefly where Janie—and Tommy, who was almost a teenager now—were these days. Last he'd heard she was living with her new husband in L.A. somewhere.

He hoped they were happy.

For reasons that weren't based on personal feelings or animosity, Lyons deliberately didn't keep track of them. The antiterrorist business, Stony Man style, made it too risky to have many friends and family. Risky on the friends and family, he amended—the woman on whose grave he now stood was living proof of that.

Living proof?

The bitter irony of the phrase struck him, and he swallowed the lump in his throat. Come to think of it, "living proof" wasn't quite right, was it? he thought bitterly. Dead proof would be more like it.

Sorry, Margie. I'm sorry you knew me. And I'm sorry it killed you.

Margie had had a kid brother, Danny, who had also joined the LAPD. Danny had wanted to be a policeman largely because he had known and admired Lyons. And he'd been a good cop, too, strong and enthusiastic and fair. He was killed in a shootout a couple of years back, and the episode had brought Lyons and Margie back together for a few months.

By coincidence, Lyons's Stony Man mission at the time had ultimately involved the same people who had killed Danny. It had added a certain measure of personal satisfaction to a job well done on a professional level.

Lyons and Margaret had begun seeing one another again.

At first it had been good. Then the same differences had reared up, and they had parted after a quarrel.

It was to be the last time he saw her alive.

She had ended up dead, her body lying in a shabby morgue in Mexico until Lyons had retrieved it and shipped it up to the States. That had been hard enough, but the hardest part of all had been the knowledge of why she had died, why they had killed her.

Lyons had hunted them down and set them straight, permanently. It hadn't brought Margaret back, of course, but it had helped put things right a little.

He laid the flowers—white roses—on the grave below the marble rectangle. Two dozen of them. The finest. Lyons wondered what Brognola or Kurtzman or some bean-counter accountant type at Stony Man Farm would think when they got the bill for that one.

Tough shit. It was the right thing to do.

Lyons stood there for several moments. It was a warm, smoggy L.A. day, but from somewhere a breeze stirred the air where he was standing.

A slight feeling of embarrassment possessed him.

He knew people sometimes said things, talked, at gravesites. It was as though they were talking to the person buried there. But Lyons didn't feel comfortable doing that. He was, or professed to be, a consummate cynic, a hard-nosed realist on the subject of death. If he was asked what happened after death, or if there was life after death, he would give a quick and ready answer.

"You die, you're dead. Nothing happens. It's over. That's it. There can't be a heaven, and I hope to shit there's no hell."

So why do you do it, Ironman? he asked himself.

Why do you come here, to this city of the dead with flowers, whenever the mission or your own time puts you in L.A.? And why do you feel better, even if it's just a little better, after you've been here?

Maybe your quick answers to the big questions are bullshit. Maybe there is something there, or you think there is. Maybe your actions speak louder than your words.

Maybe, maybe, maybe. The world was full of maybes. Fuck the maybes.

He wondered if that was his "discourse on the human condition."

Finally he cleared his throat and, still embarrassed, said aloud, "Wherever you are, Margie, I hope you're well."

The words came out in a rusty croak, but they came out.

Lyons turned and walked back to the rental car. The breeze died, and his shirt clung to his body, hot and sticky. Minutes later he passed through the big gates of the cemetery and back to the world of the present.

The dead belonged to the past, he thought, and that was over.

He lived in the present. That was where he was today. And when tomorrow came, it would be the present. And, he thought, the todays are where it's at. Today's missions. The thrill of today's dangers. The touches and scents of today's women. The hard taste of today's liquor. And, somewhere, on one of those todays, the final brutality of his own death, a bullet or a blade or a bomb with his name on it.

And, Lyons knew, when that day came—when that to-morrow became a today—he, too, would become part of the past, the past of all those who survived him.

Terra es, terram ibis, Ironman.

But for now, no more looking back. No more thoughts of Margaret, or Janie. No more of Mike Chandler, or April Rose, or Danny Williams, or Flor Trujillo, or any of the others. Each, in his or her own way, had come and gone from his life. Don't think about them, he thought. Look ahead. Bury the regrets and the maybes and the what ifs, bury them along with the bodies.

If you're lucky, you won't be reminded of any of them for quite a while.

Quite a long while, in fact.

7

Hal Brognola, the Chief of Operations for Stony Man Farm, was on the telephone, directing Blancanales and Schwarz to go to L.A. and hook up with Lyons.

"Any idea where he is, Chief?"

Gadgets was speaking into the telephone in his motel room in Seattle. Brognola was at Stony Man Farm in the mountains of Virginia outside Washington, D.C., or so Gadgets assumed. The Chief rarely got out into the field, and Gadgets had placed the call to one of the Stony Man numbers. Still, it was always possible that the guy could be anywhere, the call routed and rerouted via secure lines managed by Aaron "the Bear" Kurtzman.

As he spoke, Gadgets ran his hand through his brown hair. As Able Team's unofficial electronic and computer genius, he often had a certain rumpled look about him. It gave him just a hint of the absentminded professor type.

It was only a hint, though. At five-ten and a solid one-seventy, he was lean and fit, largely through watching his diet and knowing what his body could do. "The power of the mind," he had once kidded Lyons. The Ironman had accused Gadgets of working out in secret, expressing the opinion that nobody could stay in that kind of shape on as little exercise as Gadgets seemed to get.

And yet he did stay in shape. Damn good shape, in fact.

As Gadgets spoke, his friend and Able Team partner, Rosario Blancanales, lay sprawled on one of the beds, reading a newspaper. Or, to be more precise, scanning the headlines and captions, then reading the first paragraphs of any articles that seemed interesting.

There was quite a variety.

In Chicago somebody criticized the Reagan administration's economic policy. The critic claimed those policies had resulted in a "legacy of debt for future generations." A government spokesman responded that at least most people had jobs.

Good point, thought Pol.

In Washington, D.C., itself, somebody else predicted that the situation in Central America would develop into another Vietnam.

Blancanales, who along with Gadgets had been there and had, in fact, left a good deal of his blood on Asian real estate, saw one significant difference. Central America was a hell of a lot closer to home. Of course, that fact would also make it easier for protestors to consort with the enemy.

The so-called drug scandal among professional athletes continued unabated, and in Dallas a commission had been appointed to look into it.

So tell me something new, he thought.

Somewhere in Los Angeles a gang of professional hoodlums had robbed a family in their own home. Apparently the MO of the heavily armed robbers was to just take the place by storm, terrorize the people who lived there and cap it off by carting out all their worldly belongings, or at least the most valuable ones.

The incident had happened several days earlier—a week ago, in fact. At the time it hadn't received much coverage. But the reporter in the article compared it to several similar episodes across the country. He theorized that it could be a single gang of marauders, traveling around the country and striking when it suited them, at will and at random.

Blancanales doubted that somehow, but it could be possible.

It had been his experience that armed robberies in homes were the result of dope deals gone bad. Sometimes it involved "self-help" collection of debts from narcotics deals, or other criminal activities, that couldn't be taken into court. It was damn rare that an armed band would storm a man's castle just to pillage and loot.

Still, maybe times were changing. And if they were, it would be a hell of a scary development.

Anyway, what apparently made this particular robbery unique, even among the others profiled by the reporter, was the fact that this one had been aborted halfway through. They hadn't pulled it off. One of the family members had gotten away and called the cops, and the crooks had bailed out.

Politician frowned. He hoped the bad guys didn't think any of the victims could identify them, or it could easily be retaliation city, so to speak.

And in Seattle, where he and Gadgets were, somebody was keeping himself busy by killing prostitutes—in spite of the fact that the police thought they had caught the guy. A spokesman for the police department said that certain differences in the MO led them to believe the new killings were done by a copycat, and that their suspect in custody was still responsible for the original killings.

Probably true, thought Politician.

As he scanned the pages, Blancanales could hear the booming voice of Brognola, even though he was several feet away from Gadgets and the telephone.

"Yes, Schwarz, as a matter of fact I do know where he is," their Chief was saying. Blancanales could picture him at Stony Man Farm with his thick hair and the inevitable cigar clamped between the index and middle fingers of his right hand.

Gadgets winced and held the phone away from his ear. Brognola continued.

"He checked in with us, oh, let's see . . . yeah, day before yesterday. Called from San Diego."

"What's he up to?"

"Said he had just tried out a new kind of search warrant, whatever the hell that means."

Gadgets frowned into the phone. "Search warrant?" he repeated.

"That's what he said."

"What the hell's he doing messing around with search warrants, Chief? Is he doing a job, or maybe just having some kind of flashback to his cop days or something?"

On the bed Politician stopped scanning the paper and looked at his partner with a quizzical expression. Gadgets shrugged and waited for the response.

"I'm not clear on that, either," came the booming reply. "Except that he's not on a job. I know that much. Frankly, I was hoping you could enlighten me a little."

"Negative, Chief. I haven't seen the guy in over a week."

Brognola sighed into the phone. "And if you or Blanca-nales *did* know what it was about, I'm sure you'd tell me all about it. You wouldn't just 'back his play,' so to speak."

Brognola's voice was half serious, half mocking.

He trusted his men completely. Moreover, he knew that the bond between fighting men who hold one another's lives in their hands was both strong and necessary. And he didn't for a moment think they should spy or snitch on one another. He wouldn't want them to, in fact. Still it didn't hurt to remind each one that the acts of one could affect everyone else, and ultimately the entire Stony Man concept.

"Of course, your Excellency," Gadgets said in exaggerated deference. "I mean, of course not. I mean, the guy's my blood brother, my 'homeboy,' and we lay our asses on the line for each other all the time. But I wouldn't back his play. No, sir. Not me. Remember that when you pass out the Christmas bonuses, sir."

Brognola's laugh came back over the line. "Knock off the crap, Schwarz," he commanded.

"Yes, sir. That's a real nice tie you're wearing, too, sir," Gadgets added as a mock-fawning afterthought.

He rolled his eyes at Politician, then he covered the mouthpiece with his hand and mouthed a question, "Do you know what that psychomaniac Lyons has been up to down in 'Dago?"

Blancanales shook his head. "Not me, Homes."

"Something about a search warrant?" Gadgets prodded in the same whisper.

Politician shrugged helplessly by way of reply.

Gadgets took his hand off the mouthpiece and spoke into the phone again. "Politician says he doesn't know, either. And I'm sure he's being truthful, Chief. You can count on that, sir."

A bark of laughter boomed back over the line. "Yeah, I bet." After a pause, Brognola went on. "What's this 'homeboy' crap all about, anyway? Where'd you pick that up?"

From the bed Blancanales grinned.

The "homeboy crap" had started as a gag one day, calling each other "Homes" and "homeboys" in the manner of Californian Latino street gangsters. It was sort of the *West Side Story* of the eighties.

"Hey, maaan," Gadgets responded in the raspy voice of a street punk. He was good at imitations, a natural mimic, and the resulting voice could have been that of any knife-wielding *vato* from the barrios. "Where you been, man? A homeboy, you know, he's your *man*, dude. He's your *brother*, you know?"

"Yeah." Brognola didn't sound too impressed. "Well, anyway, this search warrant business concerns me a little. It's something I intend to explore with the lad at the earliest opportunity."

"Why so, Chief?" inquired Gadgets, dropping the accent.

"Publicity. That's why."

"What do you mean?"

"Well, it doesn't exactly serve the interests of Stony Man for its operatives to get involved in anything that could call public attention to themselves. Search warrants mean cops, and the media is always interested in police work. The last thing we need is the smiling face of one of Stony Man's finest plastered all over the ten o'clock news."

"Aren't you mixing your media, Chief?" inquired Gadgets pointedly, knowing full well he was. "I mean, with all due respect, sir, strictly speaking, one doesn't *plaster* something on video, does one? In other words—"

"Enough!" came the genial command. "How's Seattle?"

"Fine, Chief. Why?"

"Because I'm sure you'll like Los Angeles just as much."

"Los Angeles?" echoed Gadgets, who in fact had grown up in Pasadena, just outside L.A. "That place with all the smog?"

"The same. I want you there tomorrow. Check into a motel."

"The Westin Bonaventure," agreed Gadgets with a wink at Blancanales. Surprisingly Brognola didn't lodge an objection.

"Whatever," he said, apparently distracted by some other thought. "Just touch base and let me know where you're staying. No, come to think of it, I need to know now, so I can tell Lyons. What's the name of this place? The Western Buenavista?"

"Bonaventure," Gadgets corrected. "The *Westin Bonaventure*."

"It's in L.A.? The city itself?"

Aware that Blancanales was watching him intently, Gadgets responded carefully. He was trying to be casual enough so that Brognola wouldn't get suspicious until he was committed.

"Yeah. It's on Figueroa, South Figueroa, that is. It's a nice place, clean and all. You know. Friendly people. Pretty quiet, too."

"One of those little family-operated places?" asked Brognola, though his mind was obviously still on other things. Without waiting for an answer, he went on. "Well, that sounds fine. I'll take your word for it. The Westin Bonaventure. Go ahead and check in there. I'll tell Lyons to meet you tomorrow evening, as soon as he can get there."

"Ten-four, Chief," said Gadgets, his manner still elaborately offhanded.

From the bed Blancanales's face lit up in a broad grin. He, too, had grown up in and around L.A., and he knew the city well. And he also knew the Bonaventure, though not from his youth—he had stayed there a couple of years ago in the company of a certain lady, he recalled.

In fact, the Westin Bonaventure couldn't be farther from the sort of small, family-run motor lodge image that Gadgets had created and Brognola had apparently swallowed. Near downtown L.A., it was ultramodern and elegant, with tall, cylindrical towers of glistening, mirrorlike glass. It also, he knew, happened to have a hell of a good restaurant on the top floor, some thirty-odd stories above the city.

Unless things had changed a lot, he also knew that the prices were predictably a hell of a lot higher than what the Chief probably envisioned for some little motor lodge.

"Anything we should be thinking about, Chief?" Gadgets said into the phone.

Brognola hesitated. When he finally spoke, it was to deflect the question. "What do you mean?"

"You got a job for us?"

"We may have one in the offing."

Gadgets frowned. The Stony Man operations officer seemed unusually preoccupied. In fact, that was probably how they had been able to blow the Bonaventure by him. "Anything you'd like to, uh, share with us about it, Chief?"

Again Brognola paused. Then he replied crisply, "Negative. It's premature at this point. Get to L.A. and make contact at 1600 hours tomorrow. Got that?"

"Yes, sir, Chief. That's 4:00 p.m. When you talk to Lyons, tell him that's when Mickey's short arm is on the four and his long arm is on the twelve. He sometimes has difficulty telling time, you know."

After Brognola hung up, Gadgets turned to Politician, a thoughtful expression on his face.

"What is it, amigo?" inquired Pol. "We got a mission?"

"No. I mean, yeah, I guess so, but I don't know what it is yet."

"He give you any clue?"

"Negative. He seemed kind of strange, though."

"What about?"

Gadgets shook his head slightly. "Hard to tell really. He seemed real ambivalent on this one, like he couldn't make up his mind about something."

"Any idea what? Just can't decide whether to send us in, or something?"

"I don't know. He just seemed preoccupied. And that bit about Lyons seemed a little out of character, too."

Blancanales thought for a moment. "Think the mission has something to do with Carl? Something like that?"

"I don't have a clue." The face of Able Team's computer and electronics genius was furrowed in thought. Finally he shrugged and said, "Well, we'll know tomorrow, I guess."

"Maybe," agreed Politician. "Hell, who knows? It could be anything." He gestured at the newspaper. "Maybe he wants us to find the guy who's killing all the hookers."

"You never know. Oh, well," Gadgets shrugged, "Bonaventure, here we come."

At that Blancanales's face lit up in a wide grin.

His smile, and the numerous variations it had, formed a large part of the reason his nickname was Politician. He had always been able to flash an easy, charming smile at a moment's notice. "It's like a politician's, except Blanc's is real," as one person, a woman, once observed a long time ago.

A rumor existed that Blancanales had been audited once, back before the Stony Man operation had evolved into what it was today.

The IRS rep was a young woman, attractive but all business in her approach to filling Uncle Sam's coffers. And though Politician was as patriotic as the next person, his record-keeping was somewhat less than meticulous. The result was that he usually *over*paid his taxes, although he couldn't prove it.

The auditor, though, wasn't impressed. Not at first, anyway. Or, if she was, she didn't show it. Business was, after all, business.

The audit took several sessions. Each time, the broad-shouldered ex-Black Beret with the easy smile that lit up his whole face returned with more records and receipts.

Each time, the auditor reminded herself where her duty lay. The muscular, dark-complexioned man with the mysterious job, with the strong, aquiline features and hair turning a startling, premature gray, was just another number on a case file to her.

Sure.

As the audit progressed, she realized there were, of course, two sides to every issue, even an audit. People did lose their records. And, after all, the tax laws were awfully complicated.

She also began to notice the smile. Far from just "coming on" to her, as a lot of her cases did—or tried to—this guy seemed genuinely friendly, charming in a nonpushy way.

After a while, she began to wonder why he *hadn't* come on to her.

The audit proved very successful for Blancanales, however. In fact, it became clear that he had overpaid rather than underpaid. In fact, given his expenses and deductions, the government had overwithheld from his salary.

Moreover, at the conclusion of the audit, the lady IRS agent decided she had overwithheld in another area as well....

"What is it?" asked Gadgets, seeing his partner's grin at the mention of the hotel.

"The Bonaventure? He okayed that?"

"You heard him. Said fine. Lyons is supposed to meet us there tomorrow."

"Wait until he sees the bill."

Gadgets cocked his head to one side, then shrugged. "We'll cross that bridge when we come to it."

"Or *burn* that bridge."

"Whichever."

THE FIRST THING THEY DID when they arrived in L.A. was pick up their weapons.

Actually that had been arranged before they'd left Seattle.

The Stony Man operation existed in a sort of limbo, officially speaking. It wasn't part of the government, to be sure, though many if not most of the missions came from the government or involved national security in one way or another.

An important part of Stony Man consisted of what were sometimes called "the irregulars." These were an informal cadre of men and women all over the country who worked at regular jobs, but stood available to help out on an ad hoc basis, whenever the need arose.

The list included people in all sorts of professions.

Doctors were a biggie, to handle the eventuality that an operative might find himself in a strange city, wounded and in need of medical care. In such cases the laws that required reporting little things like gunshot wounds to the police could jeopardize a mission, or at least raise a battery of questions the agent would rather not have to answer.

Undertakers were also helpful, for obvious reasons.

Firearms dealers and weaponsmiths comprised another important category. Ditto dealers in cars, motorcycles, planes and boats.

But the list of irregulars wasn't confined to persons whose particular occupation could come in handy. It also included trusted people who could be called upon for tasks other than those related to their jobs. Pick somebody up at Point A and transport him to Point B, no questions asked.

Have a rental car waiting at a certain location. Call this number and give this message, quick....

All the irregulars had been checked out thoroughly. Some of them would never be called upon. Those who were would receive a call or follow-up visit from somebody official any time they were actually used.

Los Angeles wasn't a problem as far as irregulars were concerned.

After hanging up the phone with Brognola, Gadgets had called the Bear, Aaron Kurtzman. After the ritual of exchanging insults, Gadgets had dropped the problem in the Bear's burly lap, along with the shopping list of weaponry they wanted.

Now, as he and Blancanales walked toward the airport baggage claim area, Gadgets heard the page over the PA system. It wasn't his true name, of course, but the cover name he was traveling under.

"Stevens, eh?" he had said when he had read the name on the complete set of ID he had been given back at Stony Man Farm.

The technician who had created them, an expert forger, had nodded. The name, of course, was a real one, real in the sense that either a "Stevens" actually existed, or a phony one had been registered with the Department of Motor Vehicles in case somebody went behind the driver's license and checked the actual records.

"Stevens," Gadgets had mused. "Sounds like a goddamn lawyer's name, or maybe a brain surgeon. So I guess I'll have to look like a fucking Stevens for a while. Of course," he had added as an afterthought, "the real Stevens should be glad to look like me, actually."

The page directed him to pick up a courtesy phone. When he picked up the receiver, a voice he had never heard before spoke to him.

"Mr. Stevens, sir, there's a rental car waiting for you at parking level 3D. It's a gray Taurus. The key is on top of the right front wheel. I believe you'll find it's fully equipped the way you specified, sir."

The voice was young, efficient, well modulated. Gadgets suspected the irregular it belonged to had military connections, or was maybe a cop.

"Thank you. Anything else I should know about?"

"Negative, sir."

"Well, thanks again."

"Yes, sir. Good luck, Mr. Stevens."

Gadgets hung up and turned back to Blancanales. His partner wore a questioning look. Gadgets nodded, and the two men went to claim their baggage. Twenty-five minutes later they were at the car.

It was, they found, equipped as they had specified.

As far as the car went, that meant air-conditioning. But the most important part of the equipment didn't concern the vehicle. Not directly, anyway.

"Let's see what we've got, amigo," muttered Blancanales. He was standing by the trunk while Gadgets stooped and retrieved the key. Gadgets tossed it to him, and Politician opened it up.

A blanket, folded about two and a half by four feet or so, lay in the trunk. He lifted the top layer of it and inspected what lay below.

"All there?" asked Gadgets softly. He stood casually by the trunk, using his body and his suitcase to shield the contents of the trunk from anybody else in the immediate area.

"Looks like it. Let's see. What'd you ask for, again?"

"Sawed-offs, MAC-10s and Government Models."

"Well, here are the sawed-offs at least." Blancanales surveyed the weaponry concealed by the blanket.

Shotguns, three of them, twelve-gauge pumps sawed off to a maneuverable and highly illegal length.

"And the MAC-10s," he added as his gaze found the blunt, stubby, stamped-metal machine pistols.

"They .45s?" inquired Gadgets, referring to the fact that the MAC-10 came in both .45 and 9 mm versions.

Blancanales checked. "That's affirmative."

Leaning into the trunk, Blancanales made a further inspection of the weapon. The MAC-10 was normally made semiauto only. This one had an anonymous selector switch that indicated it had, in fact, been what they specified, namely a fully automatic model. Several loaded clips of ammunition—three for each one—were present as well.

"And here are the handguns," Politician continued.

Three pistols, standard Government Model Colt .45 semiautomatics. Little by little, Able Team had come around to seeing the benefit of the workhorse .45 as a close-quarter side arm. Even Lyons, who thanks to his cop days, traditionally preferred a revolver such as a Colt Python or a Smith & Wesson Model 19, had grudgingly agreed to the change.

The .45 was a hell of a man-stopper. The ammo was inter-changeable with the MAC-10, and if everybody carried the same guns, they could use one another's as well.

Blancanales handed one of the .45s to Gadgets. Then, still leaning into the trunk, he picked up the second one and checked it.

Clip full, one in the chamber. He set the safety, then slid the weapon into his waistband on the right side, butt forward, and pulled his loose-fitting shirt down over it, outside his pants.

This way he could get to the weapon with either hand, either by reaching across his body with the left, in a cross-draw mode, or with his right by turning his palm out and taking hold of the pistol grip.

Gadgets did the same thing. The two men hoisted their suitcases into the trunk. Just as Blancanales was about to slam it shut, his gaze fell on something else.

He checked it out.

"You ask for handcuffs?" he said over his shoulder to Gadgets.

"Negative. Why? Are there some there?"

"Three sets. Peerless. Your basic cop handcuffs. I wonder why these are here. We're not going to be arresting anybody, are we?"

Gadgets shrugged. "Who knows? Maybe the Bear ordered them, or maybe the irregular just threw them in for good measure."

Blancanales tossed the cuffs back into the trunk, then slammed the lid shut. As they moved around the car, Politician to the driver's side and Gadgets to the passenger's, the latter spoke suddenly.

"Say, Homes."

"*¿Sí, amigo?*"

"This is just like Christmas." Gadgets grinned and indicated the .45 on his hip. "And to think we got everything we wanted, and then some, in fact."

"Everything we asked for, you mean. Not everything we wanted."

Puzzled, Gadgets wrinkled his brow. "What do you mean? You should have said something, Homes. What else did you want?"

"A babe and a bottle."

Gadgets grinned. "Touché. Next time we talk to the Bear, we'll see if he's got an irregular who can set that up. Now let's get going before the L.A. traffic goes from bad to worse.''

"*Sí, amigo.* Next stop, the Bonaventure.''

"Ten-four.''

8

They almost didn't make it.

Even at 2:00 p.m. the traffic on the freeways to and from the airport was starting to build. Both men knew that in another hour it would be the bumper-to-bumper, stop-and-go stuff that made L.A. infamous.

Then, to make matters worse, the Taurus began to develop an engine problem.

"Shit," muttered Blancanales. "What's the matter with this *chingauzo*? It's a brand-new car."

"What's wrong?"

"Goddamn thing is overheating."

"How bad?"

Politician pointed at the gauge. The needle was pegged over to the far right, pointing at the H. Gadgets saw it, then reached over and switched off the air conditioner to take some of the load off the engine.

"Think it'll make it if the a.c.'s off?" he inquired, rolling down his window. Blancanales followed suit.

As if the car had been listening and decided to answer Politician, it provided the response. With a hiss, a puff of steam came from beneath the hood.

Gadgets saw it and gave a rueful chuckle. "Well, I guess that answers that."

Blancanales nodded. "I'm gonna grab the next off-ramp. Probably just a hose problem. Maybe just low on coolant."

"Or the thermostat, or the radiator, or water pump, or who knows what else," muttered Gadgets. Mechanically gifted as he was, he could probably rebuild an engine blindfolded if he had to.

They cruised down the next off-ramp. At the bottom of the ramp but on the opposite corner was a gas station. Politician braked at the stop sign. Then, when the coast looked clear of traffic, he eased forward, nursing the overheated machine across the intersection toward the station.

"Look out!"

Gadgets shouted the warning. Out of nowhere a car came flying down on them, along the surface street they were crossing.

It came from their right, or Gadgets's side. It was a Dodge Charger, an old one, probably late sixties or so, with a fast-back design to the body. Most of it was painted primer gray, with a few spots of flat black thrown in for good measure.

Gadgets recalled that Chargers were damn fast cars in their day, one of the "muscle cars" of the sixties. If his memory served him correctly, they came with a 440-cubic-inch engine, hemi head. With a four-barrel carburetor—or, if you were real serious, three deuces or dual fours—it was truly a screamer. Top end probably a hundred and sixty or so, easy.

This one, of course, was long past its prime. The roar of the engine sounded rough and unhealthy, the product of too many years and too much neglect.

Politician looked over to where Gadgets was pointing.

Off to their right, the surface street crowned at the top of a slight rise. The high point was some fifty yards from the stop sign at the bottom of the ramp. The Dodge crested the rise and became airborne for a few feet before crashing back to the pavement.

A shower of sparks flew from beneath the vehicle where the undercarriage smashed against the pavement. The engine roared and tires screeched.

Then, slewing wildly from side to side in a fishtail motion as the driver fought for control, the Dodge bore down on the Taurus, headed straight for a broadside against Gadgets's door.

"Shit!" Blancanales yelled.

"No shit!" Gadgets barked his agreement.

Politician stomped the accelerator to the floor. Tires yelped, and the Taurus leaped forward with surprising speed, given its struggling engine.

For a moment it looked as if they might make it.

The Charger started to turn toward its left, so as to pass behind them. The two Able Team warriors could see the driver frantically cranking the wheel. Then the tires on the Dodge lost their grip, and it started to slide.

With the scream of tortured rubber on pavement, the old Dodge slid toward them, leading with its right front fender. Then, despite the spirited attempt of the Taurus to get out of the way, the Charger clipped it on the right rear quarter panel, just behind the rear wheel.

"Shit!"

The oath tore from Politician's throat as the impact jerked them around and hurled them spinning, end around end, across the intersection.

"No shit!" echoed Gadgets.

Then, an instant later, the car banged up against the curb on Blancanales's side. It rocked as if to go over, then steadied and came to rest.

The Charger hadn't fared as well.

Gadgets twisted around in his seat, just in time to see it wrap itself around a telephone pole almost directly across the street from where the Taurus had come to rest. The drawn-out screech of rubber on pavement was chopped short by the metallic crash as the driver's door of the old car hit the pole. Gadgets felt a twinge of regret; a hell of a way for a tough car to end up.

Blancanales leaned forward and turned the ignition key off to give the tortured power plant a rest at last. Then he turned to Gadgets.

"You okay, amigo?"

"Yeah. Just fucking fine. I like how you take care of the car before you ask about your friend, though."

Politician grinned. "First things first, Homes."

"Swell."

"Hey, man. The car's okay, or at least it's been taken care of and you're okay. Now maybe we ought to see about those assholes." He jerked his head in the direction of the Charger.

"*These* assholes, you mean," corrected Gadgets, turning back and looking toward the Dodge.

"What do you mean?"

"*Those* assholes have become *these* assholes. We've got company, Homes, and do they look pissed off!"

Blancanales turned to look.

Three men had emerged from the Charger and had dashed across the street. Two of them had pistols in their hands; the third was carrying a pillowcase. The cloth bulged at irregular intervals near the bottom as if it contained something. Even as Politician turned around, the three were just about at the Taurus.

"Aw, shit," he moaned, removing the key from the ignition and slipping it into his trouser pocket as he spoke.

"No shit," agreed Gadgets.

The first of the three men to reach them was evidently the leader. He was tall and had red hair and a scraggly red beard. Above the beard his skin was pockmarked. His eyes burned, the pupils narrow and constricted, like pinpoints. The sour odor of sweat surrounded him like a cloud.

He held a revolver in his right hand.

The gunman raised the revolver and pointed it straight at Blancanales's face. It was a Smith & Wesson, Politician realized, the service revolver that took the old .45 long Colt cartridge.

On either side of the barrel, he could see the soft gray noses of the rounds in the cylinder.

"Out of the car, assholes!" the man shouted.

Politician cringed and shrank away from the man.

"I said, get out of the fucking car!" Redbeard roared.

Politician could see little dried flecks of white spittle in the corners of the man's mouth, a nauseating complement to the scummy tartar in the cracks between his teeth.

Blancanales raised his arms in a gesture that was half shrug, half supplication. "No Englich," he said. "*Por favor, señor. No* speack Englich."

"Fuck!" Redbeard grabbed the door handle and yanked, but the door was locked.

Enraged, he slammed the butt of his pistol on the roof of the Taurus. The clang reverberated through the car.

"Fuckin' wetback!" the man screamed, beside himself in a drug-induced frenzy. "Unlock the door, you beaner bastard! Get out of the fucking car, man! You don't need English to get outta the fucking car!"

Blancanales fumbled with the door lock. Then it was unlocked, and Redbeard yanked it open. On the other side of the car, the passenger side, the second gunman was doing the same thing, reaching in and hauling Gadgets out by the arm.

At that point, a series of swift and unpleasant events began happening to the gunmen.

Rather than resist the pull of the man on his side, Gadgets went with it. Using his body to block Redbeard's view, should he be looking across, Gadgets moved in quickly and kneed the gunman in the groin.

Simultaneously, using his left hand, he grabbed the revolver that was in the man's right hand.

It was a good knee job. Solid. Well placed. And it had all the momentum of Gadgets's wiry strength—not to mention his one hundred and seventy or so pounds—behind it.

"Uuhhh!"

The sound came out as a wheezing grunt. The man folded up in front of Gadgets, whose viselike grip on the revolver kept the cylinder immobilized so that it couldn't be fired.

Then the Able Team man reached into his waistband and drew his .45. Time to really get this guy's attention, he thought.

Making sure it was still locked—the safety catch on, in other words—and with his index finger outside the trigger guard, Gadgets smacked the bent-over man on the side of the head with the flat of the weapon.

It wasn't hard enough to knock the man out, but it did the trick in terms of getting his attention.

Gadgets put his face next to the gasping man's. "It's not nice to yank people out of their cars, asshole!" he said softly. "Don't do it, again! Now give Uncle Hermann your gun."

With a powerful twist of his wrist, Gadgets wrenched the pistol from the gunman's hand, breaking the man's trigger finger in the process.

On the other side of the car, Redbeard had hauled Blancanales out and had shoved him aside. Guy looks stocky enough he thought, but he lets himself be shoved aside like

some fucking pansy. With a grunt of satisfaction, Redbeard tossed his pistol onto the front seat and clambered
inside the car. The pistol bounced off the seat and into the
passenger footwell.

"Get in, you assholes!" he yelled to his companions.

Then he reached forward to start the engine.

No keys.

"The keys!" he screamed. "Gimme the keys, you wetback greaser!"

Blancanales shrugged helplessly. "No Englich, *señor...*"
he began.

Redbeard opened his mouth to scream again. Then a look
of understanding crossed Blancanales's face.

"Ah, the keys," he said.

"Yeah, the keys, you beaner! Gimme the fucking keys!"

Blancanales reached in the direction of his pocket. As he
did so, he spoke to the wired-up gunman.

"You must mean the ignition keys, don't you, sir. The
ones that activate the starter motor to turn the engine over.
Why didn't you say so? Here they are, asshole."

Politician's hand came out with the .45 Government
Model.

Taking a quick stride forward, he reached in the open
window with his left hand and grabbed a handful of dirty
red hair. Then he yanked the face toward him and at the
same time jammed the muzzle of the pistol into the man's
ear.

"Here are the fucking keys, white boy!" he hissed. "It's
the closest thing to a key you're gonna see!"

Swiftly he let go of the man's hair and yanked open the
door. Then he grabbed the stunned gunman by the hair once
again and dragged him out of the car. Using the incredible
strength of his stocky frame, Politician swung the gunman
around and slammed him over the hood of the Taurus.

On the opposite side of the car, Gadgets performed a similar maneuver with his new playmate. The man appeared unable to decide which hurt more: the nausea in his balls or the shooting pain in his index finger.

Near the rear of the Taurus was the third man.

He stood stock-still, gaping at the unexpected turn of events. He was a scrawny specimen with long stringy brown hair and tattoos on both forearms. He still clutched the lumpy pillowcase, but he seemed incapable of movement, as though his mind were unable to take in what his eyes were seeing.

He had started to go around to the passenger side, to get in with the second gunman. Then, seeing matters take such a disastrous turn, he had simply stopped as if paralyzed.

Now he turned as if to run.

"Freeze!"

The command came at him in stereo. Two voices, speaking in unison. At the same time twin .45s were turned in his direction. They were leveled at him, steadied and held there.

"I know what you're thinking, asshole," began Gadgets.

"I don't," said Politician, his brow furrowed, as if perplexed. "What's he thinking, amigo?"

"He's thinking, 'Will these guys really shoot me in the back if I just drop the bag and start running.' Yep, that's what he's thinking, all right. I'd bet a lunch on it."

"Is that really what you're thinking, amigo?" Blancanales asked the frightened man.

The man's mouth opened and shut, but nothing came out except bad breath.

Gadgets supplied the answer. "Yep. That's it. And right now he's talkin' himself into thinking he won't. Isn't that right, scumbag? You're telling yourself we won't shoot a fleeing man in the back. Right?"

He waited, but the gaping man didn't speak.

"Well, guess what?"

The hood still didn't speak.

"Ding!" Gadgets pretended to look at his watch. "Time's up. You didn't make a guess, so I'll answer for you. The answer is 'yes.'"

"'Yes' what?" asked Politician.

"Yes, we'd shoot him in the back."

Blancanales looked at his partner in mock surprise. "It is? We would?"

Gadgets wrinkled his brow. "Well...yeah," he replied hesitantly. "Isn't it? Wouldn't we?"

"If this guy drops the money and just hauls ass, you'd shoot him? In the back?"

"Sure. Why not?"

"Is it legal?" persisted Blancanales.

"Who knows?"

Politician looked over to the sidewalk. A small crowd of people had begun to assemble: a couple of gas jockeys from the service station, a tall, broad-shouldered young man wearing a work shirt with the name Presidential Nursery, and a handful of other onlookers. They stood beyond the sidewalk on the paved apron of the gas station.

Blancanales grinned and spoke to the crowd. "Anybody know the answer to that? Is it legal for us to shoot this dude in the back if he runs?"

Nobody answered.

"Anybody here mind if we do?"

This time a couple of the onlookers grinned. The young man in the nursery shirt shouted, "Hell, no!"

Politician turned back to Gadgets. "Well, they don't care if we do, but I still don't know if it'd be legal."

"Who cares?"

"Well..." began Blancanales in mock hesitation.

"Look," his partner said, "the fuckers just probably pulled an armed robbery. And they just tried to rob us of our car. I don't see a gun on this guy, but he's with two guys who do have guns."

"Did have guns," amended Politician.

Gadgets nodded. "Did have guns. So it's reasonable to assume he's armed, too. Probably has his gun in his back pocket, in fact."

Blancanales pretended to consider the argument. Finally he nodded. "Yeah, I guess you're right. Okay. You can shoot him if he runs."

"What about you?" inquired Gadgets.

"Me?" Blancanales seemed surprised.

"Yeah. Are you gonna shoot him if he runs? Or is it just gonna be me?"

"*Sí, amigo.* Of course I'll shoot him. There was never any question about *me*. It was you I was wondering about. I just had to test you." He paused, then added, "I'd give the bastard a chance, though."

"How so?"

"I'd hold the pistol in my left hand."

"But you're left-handed," Gadgets protested.

"No, I'm not," insisted Blancanales.

"Are, too."

"Am not. Not really, anyway."

"Well, you're ambidextrous."

"So?"

In the distance sirens wailed. The two Able Team men suddenly looked at each other in consternation. "Remember what the Chief said about Lyons and the search warrant?" Gadgets began.

"Right. No publicity. We gotta haul ass."

"What'll we do with these guys?"

They looked at each other. Then Gadgets said, "We really can't shoot 'em. Not now, anyway. And we can't let 'em go, either. If only we had . . ." Then it dawned on both men at the same moment.

"The handcuffs!"

Blancanales turned to the gas jockey, the one who had agreed to shooting the robber. "Could you put some water in this thing, amigo? Pronto?"

The gas jockey just stared at him. Blancanales was getting ready to repeat his question when another voice spoke up.

"I'll do it." The voice belonged to the guy in the Presidential Nursery shirt. He looked about twenty, tall and strong. The name on his work shirt said Wes. He stepped forward from the crowd. "What's the problem with it, anyway?"

"Damn thing is overheating. If you can just fill it, we can get out of here and get to someplace else where we can really check it out."

"Sure thing." Wes hurried over to the car.

"Use a towel to open it—it's pretty hot."

"Got it."

Politician turned and walked rapidly to the trunk of the car. He unlocked it and pried it open—the hinges had bent from the impact. He found the three pairs of cuffs.

Less than a minute later the three robbers were back inside the Charger. They were in the rear seat, their hands cuffed behind their backs, arms interlocked with one another.

"Three drugged-out losers without enough brain cells among them to make the intelligence of a stump," Gadgets observed.

Working rapidly, they tossed the two pistols into the trunk.

"And now the pillowcase," Blancanales said. He dumped its contents into the trunk. Several packets of bills, along with maybe fifty or so loose bills of varying denominations, fell into the trunk. He inspected one of the packets. It had a paper band that bore the name First Fidelity Bank of Los Angeles.

"Just as I thought," observed Gadgets.

The wail of sirens grew louder. Politician took the keys to the Charger and threw them into the trunk, then slammed the lid down. Then they sprinted back to the Taurus.

"Thanks, Wes," said Blancanales. "You are Wes, right?" he added, realizing the shirt could belong to somebody else.

"Wes Conwell," the man nodded. "It was out of water, so I filled it. I didn't see any obvious leaks, but they might not show up until it's under pressure. Say," Wes added, "is there some reason you're trying to get out of here before the cops get here?"

"Yeah." Politician hesitated, then lowered his voice. "We're federal agents on a secret assignment."

"What do you want me to tell the cops?" Wes asked.

"The truth. Tell 'em what we looked like. Tell 'em what I've just told you. We just can't hang around, that's all."

"Gotcha."

"Thanks, pal."

Blancanales slid behind the wheel of the Taurus. He heard Wes's voice and turned around.

"Yeah?"

Wes stood there with a grin on his face. "If they get out and start running, is it okay if *I* shoot 'em?"

Blancanales grinned and gave the thumbs-up gesture. "It's okay with me," he shouted, "but the law might disapprove of it."

The Taurus started right up. The needle pegged right again to the H, then began to swing the other way as the cooling water was pumped through the block.

With a scream of tires, they pulled onto the freeway on-ramp just as the police cars crested the rise behind them.

9

After three hours of tossing and turning, Hal Brognola admitted defeat.

The glowing red digits of his bedside clock cast a pale soft light against the wall of his room at Stony Man Farm. The clock read 2:07, Eastern Standard Time. In the frequent intervals he had checked it since going to bed, the Chief had seen the numbers wink inexorably upward as the time crawled toward its present reading.

He switched on the light by the bed, then got up and found a robe. It was a tattered brown terry cloth affair, sagging and comfortable, and he cinched it around his waist. Finally, slipping his feet into well-worn slippers, he padded down the corridors of the Stony Man building.

Minutes later, a cup of steaming hot milk in his right hand, he ambled to the sitting room area that overlooked the Virginia hills. He made his way to his favorite chair, his "thinking chair," and sat down.

In his left hand Brognola held a single manila folder. It contained perhaps eight or ten sheets of paper, neatly secured to the right-hand side of the file by a paper clip at the top. In addition, gripped against the file on the outside, were two or three assorted papers. They consisted of a handwritten letter, its envelope and some miscellaneous notes jotted on notepaper.

It was these documents that had caused his concern.

Brognola took a sip of the milk and sighed. Though he felt okay right now, he also knew that later that day, by two or three o'clock in the afternoon, the lack of sleep would make itself known.

Am I getting too old for all this? he wondered.

It should have been a simple enough problem, a routine business decision. Just look at the facts and then decide if Able Team should be put on this case or not. And, in this instance, that meant looking at it from a couple of different aspects.

The first was whether it was something he felt came within the parameters of the Team's mandate, something covered by what had become known as the Stony Man Doctrine.

He had to say yes to that one. Not just yes, but hell, yes. Without a doubt. No sweat.

The second question was the more difficult one. Even if the answer to the first one was yes, should he still put Able Team on it, given the peculiar, one-in-a-million coincidence that this case involved?

Under other circumstances, if the Stony Man enterprise undertook the job, it would be right up Able Team's alley. In the years that Stony Man had been in operation, a sort of de facto specialization had developed among its various operatives.

Among the two main teams, Able Team and Phoenix Force, a division of labor of sorts had emerged.

Though there were exceptions, these days Brognola liked to use Phoenix for the international jobs. The stateside work he preferred to shunt in the direction of Able Team.

He supposed that part of it had to do with the backgrounds of the men who made up each team. In a sense, Phoenix Force had a more international cast of characters, being a mixture of commandos and agents—not to say misfits, he thought with amusement—from several different countries.

Able Team, on the other hand, was especially suited to combating domestic terrorism. Between the three of them, four if you included Lao Ti, there was virtually no setting they couldn't weasel their way into. And Lyons's unique background, first as an L.A. street cop and later as a member of a federal organized crime strike force, opened a number of official and quasi-official doors stateside; his contacts would have been wasted, or at least underutilized on the international front.

Brognola sighed. Ironically it was Lyons who was the cause of his present concern.

It had all begun straightforwardly enough.

Brognola turned his attention to the manila file. The tab along the top edge read MARAUD 040687.

The digits stood for the opening date of the file. Usually this was the date of the first communication received by Stony Man Farm regarding a case. The word MARAUD identified the operation by a key word that seemed to fit the mission.

Brognola forced his mind to go over the contents of the folder once more.

It wasn't that he didn't already know what the file contained. Instead, he hoped that by rambling through it yet again he might come up with another approach, a solution that had heretofore eluded him.

The contents of the file were in reverse chronological order. This meant the most recent items were right on top. In this instance, of course, there weren't many items in the file as yet.

Brognola went to the bottom of the file, the first notations on the case.

It began with his own handwritten notes, dated April 7. He had received a telephone call from a man in the Justice Department. In Brognola's usual careful style, the notes didn't contain the man's name, or even that he worked for Justice.

There was a reason for that. A couple of reasons, actually.

Brognola's theory was that files were a means, not an end. Files were kept for a reason, or to satisfy some specific need or needs. If you were a doctor, he reasoned, you would keep files of pertinent information on the patient's illnesses. But you didn't put in what he told you about his golf swing, or his sex life, unless those things happened to be relevant to the problem or the treatment.

In other words, the rule was that the only things that should be put into a file were items that related to the problem or the solution.

In the case of Stony Man Farm, two considerations governed what went into the manila folders. One was their purpose. The other consisted of the need for security. Both factors dictated that the actual "hard copy" notes be as brief and as cryptic as possible, and that any information that could compromise security be omitted or encoded.

In Brognola's mind, the only reason he kept a file was to help him manage the case.

"Memory props," he called them. "That's all they are, memory props. I'm not keeping a diary, or writing a goddamn book."

If an item of information, a bit of data, would help jog his memory regarding some aspect of the case, it went into the file. If it didn't, it got shredded. And surprisingly, his working rule was that if he didn't know if he should keep a particular item, he got rid of it.

"When in doubt, rip it out," the head Fed always said.

This kept the files lean. No names of anybody except targets, and even some of those were in code, depending on the sensitivity of the case. And, with respect to names and any other material, the files included only such identifying information as was absolutely necessary to act as Brognola's "memory prop."

This approach also served the second consideration, namely, the maintenance of security.

"Just exactly what are you afraid might happen?" Kurtzman had inquired once when Brognola had expressed this concern. The Bear was generally allowed the same information about the overall operation as Brognola, even though he didn't make operational decisions. This was due to his indispensable genius in the area of computers and intelligence gathering.

"Why make it easy for them?" Brognola replied cryptically.

Kurtzman considered that. "I realize that if someone accessed our files, we wouldn't want every detail laid out in large print. But who the hell could ever get to them? It's not exactly as if we've got the public wandering in and out of the place, you know."

"Remember the day of mourning?" Brognola's voice was quiet, solemn, as if concealing great pain.

The Bear framed his answer as tactfully as possible. Brognola's reference was to a near-successful attack on Stony Man Farm, in which April Rose, Stony Man's mission controller, had died. "I remember," Kurtzman said softly. "I'm simply suggesting that a repeat of that isn't likely."

"True enough. But everything in life is chancy, and you know we've been attacked recently." He paused, then with a tired grin added, "I just want to be sure that if the Mafia, the Russians or a congressional committee ever got hold of our files, they'd be in for a big letdown.''

They all recognized, quite correctly, Brognola thought now, that the information contained in those files came under the heading of priceless intelligence. Moreover, it would be devastating if that data fell into the wrong hands.

For Brognola all three groups—organized crime, the Communists and Congress—fell within the category of "wrong hands."

Of course, to Brognola and Kurtzman, every action that had been taken on a case was ultimately accessible. One just had to know how to do it. And they, and only they, had that knowledge. Not even the operatives themselves—Lyons or Blancanales or Schwarz, in the case of Able Team—knew about that.

It wasn't that Brognola doubted their reliability. Their loyalty was without question. Still, it was a commonsense and hard-nosed fact that the less one knew about something, the less he could be made to tell if he fell into the wrong hands and was subjected to a combination of pain, drugs and persuasion.

Strangely this didn't offend the agents in the slightest. In fact, they took a sort of perverse pride in the practice. It emphasized the dangers of their work. And, in a peculiar sort of way, it made them even more fearless than they already were because all they had to lose was their own lives.

If that happened, of course, it wouldn't be in a blaze of glory, but in a prolonged exit of mind-bending pain.

It came with the territory. Part of the job.

The method in which Brognola and Kurtzman, the latter because of his status as an adjunct to the Chief could access additional information was through the label. In this case it was the word MARAUD.

Through the use of telephone lines and radio and micro-wave signals, the Bear was able to tap into virtually every computer system in the country. Government, private industry, banking, airlines—given enough time, the Stony Man computers could hook up.

Often they would do it without the target system being aware of what was happening. And, if somebody in charge of the infiltrated system did become aware, and tried to backtrack, all he would end up with was what looked like a foul-up with some other, independent computer system.

It was all highly illegal of course.

"I need you to commit a few felonies for me," Brognola liked to say when he dropped a search request on the Bear. "I'll send cookies to you in the penitentiary if you get caught."

"With all due respect, Chief," Kurtzman would jokingly respond, "if I go to the penitentiary, so will you."

"I'll disown you," Brognola would say with a grin. "Oatmeal cookies, isn't it? Oatmeal with raisins?"

"Chocolate chips, not raisins."

"Okay. I'll try to remember that."

No details of this kind of intelligence activity appeared in the file. However, any inquiry into the computers that had to do with that file would be made under a code word. That word was the name on the file folder, in this case, MA-RAUD, plus numerous other complicated access codes.

Thus, any step in the case could be retraced at a later date by accessing that label. And, of course, items of immediate interest or relevance could be acquired in the form of a printout—the hard copy—and put in the file.

It was just such a file that Brognola sat down to peruse that morning.

His memo of April 7 contained his own handwritten notations of the conversation with the man from Justice. Now, even as he reviewed the cryptic jottings, he could recall the telephone conversation virtually word for word.

"Good morning, Hal," his friend had said.

"Fred!" Brognola had boomed back. "Good to hear from you! How have you been?"

Even as he listened, Brognola could picture the caller. The man he called Fred—which wasn't the man's real name but a nickname Hal had given him years before when he'd worked in covert operations for the Justice Department— was one cold son of a bitch. He wore, or used to wear, steel-framed glasses. His face was squarish; come to think of it, squarish would be a good way to describe the entire man.

Yes, squarish would do nicely, Brognola recalled.

Fred was medium height, medium build, precise without being stolid, compact without being stout. The medium man—that would have been a good nickname for him. And precise. Shit, was that bastard precise. When he smiled, it was as if his features underwent a programmed mechanical process. Hold "smile" for two seconds, then return, all very precise.

Maybe the guy's not a human at all, Brognola suddenly thought for the first time. Maybe he's a cyborg—a cybernetic organism—part man and part computer.

And tough, the guy was real tough. Eyes like steel. Come to think of it, like Carl Lyons's eyes in a way. The Ironman had icy blue eyes, eyes that could be cold and without mercy. But Fred's eyes weren't as blue. They were a gunmetal gray, and they were *always* without mercy.

But whatever else you had to say about the guy, his loyalty to the U.S. in general and to the Justice Department in particular was without question. And he was a good man, one of the best, actually, to have on your side in the shark pool of national and international policy. Just the kind of guy you would want to be your negotiator with the Russians.

"Well, thank you," came the precise reply. "Yes, I've been well. How about you, Hal?"

"Fine. Great."

Brognola paused. He knew that Fred didn't really care how he had been, except insofar as it might affect whatever project was on his mind. And there had to be such a project. Fred wasn't much for keeping in touch with old colleagues, not even if the old colleague had been his most trusted associate at one time.

I wonder if the guy's got any friends, any *real* friends, the kind you could fart and tell dirty jokes with, Brognola thought suddenly. Probably not, he answered himself. Still, he's the kind of guy I'd want to have negotiating for me with the Russians.

Because he had been such a highly valued colleague of Fred's, Hal knew he could get away with kidding him a little. "So, how's your golf game?" he boomed.

Fred detested golf.

"Heh, heh, heh." Three precise expressions of mirth came back over the line. "How's your business, Hal?"

"You already know, or you wouldn't be calling me."

"Heh, heh. True enough. I have a little, ah, undertaking that might interest you."

"All right." Brognola knew that the time for jocularity was over. He kept his voice neutral. "Tell me about it, Fred."

"It's a little different from our usual problems. It seems we have a band of modern-day outlaws who've been going about breaking into people's homes and terrorizing them. Rape, pillage and plunder. That sort of thing."

"I read about it in the papers."

Fred sighed. "Ah, yes. The free press. A wonderful institution, the press. I wonder where we would be without it."

Somehow Brognola got the impression that Fred could do without the media.

"These...marauders have been running circles around the police because they're so mobile. They hit a city one night and are in a different state by the next morning."

"Hit and run," Brognola suggested.

"Precisely. It's a problem of staggering dimensions. Citizens being assaulted and robbed in their own homes. It portends a return to the Dark Ages."

Shit, thought Brognola, "portends?" The guy's a human dictionary. Why not "it's like a return to the Dark Ages." Then, in a flash of inspiration, he gave an appropriate response, something he knew Lyons would have said.

"Sounds like it really sucks in a big way."

For a moment Fred was caught off guard. Then he recovered and went on. "Ah, yes. It does, as you so eloquently put it, suck."

"What about the cops? What are they doing?"

"Given the bureaucratic and, well, parochial tendencies of our police, it's difficult for them to do more than just investigate the incident where it happened."

"What do you mean, 'parochial,' Fred? You mean like a parochial school? These guys Catholic, or something?" Brognola knew perfectly well what the man meant, but it seemed fun to keep him a little off-balance.

Except it didn't work.

"Ah, no. We have no evidence of any ties to any particular religion. No, I use the term 'parochial' in a more general sense. Restricted in thought. Narrow in scope. Provincial."

Brognola couldn't help grinning into the phone. The guy was perfect. Maybe he was a cyborg, after all. He had either missed or ignored the attempt at humor and had answered it at face value.

"I see."

"Yes. It's a problem."

"Well," said the Stony Man Chief after a few moments, "isn't that right up the FBI's alley? Can't you sic them on these guys?"

A heavy sigh came over the line. Brognola continued, however.

"I seem to recall a couple of laws that would let the FBI investigate. Give them jurisdiction over the matter. Couldn't you guys go after them for ITAR?" He pronounced it "eye-tar." "Or possibly the RICO laws?"

"You ask several questions at once," observed Fred. "And there are several answers."

"Go on," said Brognola genially.

"ITAR—Interstate Travel in Aid of Racketeering—is a possibility, of course. RICO—the Racketeer Influenced and Corrupt Organization law—would also work."

"I know what the initials mean, Fred."

"Acronym, Hal. Not initials. Acronyms."

"All right, acronyms. Whatever the hell they are. I still remember what they stand for."

"Ah, I wasn't sure."

Fred sighed. Brognola realized this was probably his idea of kidding, a hilarious jest, in fact.

"After all," the man from Justice continued, "you've been out of the department for a while. And, as I recall, you don't direct your efforts these days towards prosecution, do you? Building a case to take to court under the laws of this great land is not what you're all about these days, is it?"

"Not exactly."

"No. I didn't think so. As I recall, there is no appeal from one of your, ah, verdicts."

"No appeal on this earth," Brognola agreed. "I wouldn't know about elsewhere."

"The mysteries of the universe," Fred sighed. "We must get together some time and share our views on that. It would be fascinating, I'm sure."

"So why not the FBI?"

Fred spoke carefully. "The Bureau does good work. Excellent work, in fact. Competent and dedicated men and women."

Brognola didn't comment.

"Well, the FBI is on the case, as a matter of fact. Unfortunately, they're not well suited to combating this sort of, ah, operation."

"Why not?"

"They are always being managed by people who have no idea what fighting crime is like. Congress, for example. And the press, and even indirectly by the American Civil Liberties Union, who, I should observe, can exist only through the efforts of people like you and me."

"Tell me something I don't already know."

"As a result, the Bureau's agents are bound by all sorts of legal formalities—search warrants, judges, internal procedures, that sort of thing."

"Go on."

"Well, to use your phrase, Hal, if the enemy's tactics are 'hit and run,' the Bureau can't win if its tactics are 'wait until Congress and the ACLU approve their next move.' You see the distinction, I trust."

"I do indeed."

Fred spoke thoughtfully. "What we need, I feel, is a group that is just as mobile and, to use a term I saw on a football broadcast once, as hard-hitting as the marauders are. And, if I may say so, just as ruthless.''

"And you thought of your old buddy Hal and his little extralegal operation here in Virginia.''

"Indeed I did.''

"So, here we are.''

"Yes, Hal. Here we are. So, what do you think?''

Brognola thought it over. Then, with a half smile on his face, he took a deep breath and gave his reply. "Why don't you cut the crap, Fred old buddy, and tell me what this is really all about?''

Brognola leaned back in his swivel chair and grinned into the phone. He was enjoying himself immensely. All things considered, Fred wasn't such a bad guy. Moreover, he was one hell of a competent executive. Brognola respected him completely in terms of his ability and leadership.

But, he thought, the guy was just so emotionless, so precise and computerlike, that it was, to put it bluntly, fun to fuck with him a little.

And he had done that. Boy, had he done that.

He pictured Fred at that moment. The man did everything in neat, precise, straight lines. Right now he was probably sitting back, his face expressionless, while his mind sorted through a host of questions.

What had happened, Fred's brain would be considering.

What did Brognola mean by "cut the crap?''

Did he know there was more to the mission than Fred was letting on?

And, if so, how did he know that?

Right then, Fred would be replaying the mental tapes in his mind. He would be searching for some clue that he had let slip, something that had tipped Brognola off. And maybe Fred would find it, and maybe he wouldn't, Hal thought. In any event, it wouldn't do the man from Justice any harm to be reminded that Hal had himself been every bit Fred's equal in the strategy department.

The same held true for the ruthlessness department, despite Brognola's genial exterior.

Actually, it was precisely Fred's greatest strength that tipped Hal off. A guy like that, a human calculating machine, doesn't get all whipped up at the thought of people getting robbed in their own homes. Or, to be more accurate, he probably gets intensely offended, but, given the other problems that go with his job, he wouldn't get so angry that he'd dispatch a team of hit men to go after the guys. No, there had to be something else going on.

After a long pause the man from Justice spoke.

"Just, ah, what do you mean, Hal?" he asked, his voice without expression.

"Whaddya mean, what do I mean?" boomed Hal. The guy was fishing, he thought delightedly.

"Your words were, ah, I believe, 'Why don't you cut the crap, Fred old pal, and tell me what this is really all about.'"

"'Buddy,'" corrected Brognola.

"What?"

"I said, 'Fred old buddy,' not 'Fred old pal.'" It wouldn't hurt to put the bastard in his place a little.

"Heh, heh, heh. That's true. I was just testing you."

"Sure." Brognola paused. "As I said, why *don't* you cut the crap and tell me what else is going on."

"Why do you think anything else is going on?"

"Fred. This is me. Hal. We worked together, remember? I know how your mind works. And I also know what smells right, and what doesn't smell right. And this stinks."

"Oh? How is that?"

"Your explanation of what's going on. It stinks. Something stinks in the state of Denmark, someone in *Hamlet* put it."

"I believe, Hal, the correct quotation is, 'Something is rotten in the state of Denmark.'" Fred's voice was expressionless. Still, he was correct on his Shakespeare, Brognola realized. Chalk one up for the man from Justice.

"Whatever. Look, Fred. You laid it on too thick. A 'return to the Dark Ages,' for Christ's sake? When did you ever give a damn about that?"

"What do you mean?"

"All right, so you care about it in a general sense. But when did you ever seek the assassination of somebody under the bullshit rationale that whatever he's up to poses such a threat that it 'portends a return to the Dark Ages'?"

"Please continue, Hal. This is fascinating."

"Look. You don't send us out after guys just because they threaten the American way. Or signal a return to the Dark Ages. Hell, it would be too hard to know where to draw the line. Jesus, we'd be killing half the lawyers in the country if that were the test."

"Are you saying I don't seek to preserve democracy, Hal?"

Brognola grinned into the phone.

The guy from Justice was deliberately misinterpreting his words, a favorite tactic of attorneys and debaters. "Hell, no. I'm sure you care about that. We all do. That's why we do this thankless goddamn job. But there's got to be a more specific reason than that, or you wouldn't be going after these guys."

He paused. Fred didn't respond. Brognola waited an appropriate time, then went on.

"To put it another way, exactly how do these guys pose such a threat? I mean, I'm against robbing and pillaging in the home as much as anybody. Most people are, except maybe the courts and the lawyers. But apart from the fears of the citizens, what's going on here?"

This time there was a really long pause. Brognola was determined to wait it out. Finally Fred spoke. "Well, there are certain other considerations," he conceded at last.

"Like what?"

Fred hesitated, then spoke carefully, even more so than usual. "It seems that by chance the last place these men struck was the Los Angeles home of a man named Steve Odom. Steve was—is, I should say, a VP for a company called SanDor Corporation. He also has a Ph.D. in mathematics. SanDor was working on a government contract for a highly classified and sensitive weapons system. National defense stuff. Dr. Odom was the man in charge of the project."

"Ah, so," said Brognola in a hideous parody of the well-used oriental expression of understanding. "I begin to see shapes in the mist."

"Indeed. In any event, it seems that the night the Odom home was pillaged Dr. Odom had brought some papers home to work on."

"Classified stuff? Top secret?" interjected Hal.

"Regrettably, yes. It was a violation of security, of course."

"You're being awfully blasé about a breach of security," Hal observed. "At one time, you would have hung this guy by his balls. You getting soft in your old age?"

"Well, he's an indispensable man to the project, for one thing."

"So?"

Fred continued as if he hadn't heard the interjection. "Moreover, he has most of it in his head anyway. We can't very well stop him from taking *that* home, now can we?"

"Go on," said Brognola, ignoring what Fred probably thought was high humor.

"Well, it seems that the suspects made off with some of the papers Dr. Odom was working on."

"Wait a minute," interjected Brognola. "Wasn't that the L.A. caper? From what I read in the papers, they bailed out on that one. Didn't they get scared off?"

"That is only partially correct. They were, in fact, forced to abandon the assault midway through when Dr. Odom's wife, Jane, was able to make her escape. But they still got away with whatever had already been loaded into their vehicle."

"How does that happen to include a pile of classified files, especially since they probably looked like a bunch of equations that nobody but an expert could figure out?"

"It appears it was a chance occurrence. Apparently, one of the marauders grabbed Dr. Odom's briefcase on the way out."

Brognola thought that over. The interest of the Justice Department, through Fred, started to make more sense.

"What was in the papers?" the Stony Man Chief inquired at last.

"That is, I'm afraid, highly classified information."

"I assumed that. What was in the papers?"

Fred sighed. "I suppose I should be gratified to see that you haven't changed since we last worked together."

"What was in the papers, Freddie?"

"You are persistent to the point of becoming tiresome, Hal. It is an old failing of yours, if I may say so."

"You may. What was in the papers?"

"Well, Dr. Odom's company was doing some key research on the so-called Star Wars project, the satellite defense system proposed by the Reagan administration."

"I thought the Star Wars package was just a bluff," Brognola interjected.

"A bluff?"

"Well, the papers make it sound like it's basically a scare tactic. Make the Russians think we're on the brink of this massive death ray, then agree not to follow up with it if they stop making nukes."

"A straw man is the legal term," observed Fred.

"Whatever. Besides, I thought it was more or less history by now."

"So did a lot of people. The fact of the matter is that research by Dr. Odom's company—along with many others, both in the government and private labs—has made significant advances in the implementation of such a program. Astronomical strides, so to speak."

"Are you telling me Star Wars could work? For real? Soon?"

"That's precisely what I'm telling you."

Brognola let out a low whistle. "No shit," he said softly.

"No, ah . . . that's correct, Hal. It has the potential to put our defense capabilities decades ahead of the Soviets. It will be the best deterrent to nuclear war that the world has known."

Brognola knew exactly what the man from Justice meant.

He was a great believer in the fact that if you were big enough, and bad enough, people left you alone. That principle had occurred to him as a kid in high school when he had looked around and realized that nobody ever picked on "Tuffy" Tuagotuloa.

Tuffy was a Samoan who resembled a refrigerator with hair on top of it. The guy had had muscles all over. He had also been one of the nicest guys around, an easygoing, gentle youth. At age seventeen he was bench-pressing four hundred pounds, which was a hell of a lot of weight in those presteroid days.

Nobody ever picked on Tuffy, Hal had noted.

Even the bad guys, the punks and the "toughs," as Brognola's mother had called them, didn't. Tuffy never had to fight because it was obvious to everybody that this nice guy would reduce them to a grease spot on the road if he were ever provoked beyond his breaking point.

"Fred, are you telling me that these jerk-off thugs stole the plans to the Star Wars system?"

"Nothing so dramatic as that. The plans to the Star Wars system, as you put it, would fill volumes. Nonetheless, they are now in possession of documents that certain other national powers would find fascinating. If these papers fall into the wrong hands, the advantages to national security that Star Wars offers will be significantly reduced."

"I see," Brognola said at last.

"It is a serious problem, one which warrants resorting to extralegal means that I, of course, detest."

"Me, too," said Brognola facetiously.

"You'll undertake it, then?"

"I don't see why not."

Now, sitting in his armchair, the thinking chair, Brognola thought about the conversation that was reflected on the notes he had jotted down.

One thing was clear.

The need existed. Urban terrorist thugs who lucked into the possession of such items could threaten America's best hope at preventing the nukes from flying back and forth around the globe.

And, as the man he called Fred had observed, they couldn't wait for ordinary investigative means to catch these guys.

The means were there of course. Sic the FBI on them, maybe in combination with the U.S. Marshal's investigators and some hot local cops who could be cross-sworn as Feds. Make an ad hoc strike force like that and you'd get results. A team like that would catch these guys, and they would make sure it was a prosecutable case, too, with notebooks filled with well-written reports and files of evidence.

And, if they were lucky, it would occur sometime in the next six or eight weeks.

Too long.

Another thing was sure. If anybody could do what needed to be done, Able Team could.

True, when Able Team finished, there wouldn't be notebooks of reports and files of evidence. But then again, there wouldn't be anybody to prosecute, either.

There was only one little problem.

Brognola turned his attention to another document in the file. It was a letter, typewritten, on plain white bond. It had been addressed to Carl Lyons at an address in Washington, D.C. The address was maintained by Stony Man Farm for just such correspondence, an address that any of the operatives could pass out to family and friends.

Very little mail came there. It didn't pay to have close ties to family or friends. It was always fastest to travel alone.

The return address on both the envelope and on the top of the letter read "Dr. and Mrs. Steve Odom." The address was for their Encino home—the home that had been assaulted.

The letter was the problem. Brognola sighed and read it for perhaps the tenth time.

Dear Carl,

It feels strange to write you like this, given all the circumstances. I've started this letter a dozen times—well, three or four, anyway—and ended up throwing it away each time.

When we got the divorce, I hated you and loved you at the same time. I felt abandoned. But one of the last things you said to me was that if I ever needed any help, to call you.

I still remember how you said it. Do you, Carl? You stood there on one foot and then the other, and you finally blurted it out. "Look," you said, "I know you don't think it will ever happen, but if you ever get in a jam where you need somebody like me, I hope you'll call." And then you laughed like you were embarrassed and said, "You know, if you ever need anybody blown away or something."

I swore I'd never call on you.

I memorized those lines, and made an oath that I would never let myself take you up on it. I even used to make up scenarios in my mind, where I might be tempted to call in that marker, and then solved the problem myself without having to.

It's hard to say this now, but I need your help.

The situation is this. We, my husband, Steve, and I, are in a jam. It's a jam that the law and all the cops in the world can't help. I'm afraid we'll be killed if we don't get some help.

I'll give you the details when and if you can help. We were robbed, and Steve was hospitalized. And then I recognized one of the guys when I just by chance saw him on television, and now they're trying to kill us.

If you can't come, or if you don't want to come, I'll understand. If it was an empty promise and you never had any intention of following through with it, I'll understand.

Steve knows about this. He is in agreement that I write you, though I believe he has some misgivings.

Sincerely,
Jane Odom

P.S. Tommy is almost a teenager. He is an enthusiastic, squared-away kid—a real "mad dog." He's got the start of good shoulders on him, too, just like his biological father.

Brognola finished reading the letter again. Then he set the now-empty mug down and, with that hand, rubbed his eyes and forehead.

The letter had come as a total surprise. It had come the day after his conversation with Fred.

I can't send Lyons on this one, he thought. Christ, the man is already staggering with guilt over that Williams woman, Margaret or whatever her name was. The one who got killed in connection with that scheme to dump nuclear waste into New York City's water supply.

Lyons blames himself for her death.

Besides, even without that, you can't send a man on a life-and-death mission where the personal circumstances are so acute.

Doctors don't treat themselves or their wives. Too much personal involvement.

The lawyer who represents himself has a fool for a client and an incompetent attorney. Ditto if he tries to represent his own family. Too much personal involvement.

There's no way I can send Lyons on this. Too much personal involvement.

But right now I don't have anybody else. Hal Brognola sighed.

10

Lyons actually got to the hotel before Gadgets and Politician. He checked in and threw his suitcase on one of the beds. Then he kicked off his shoes to feel the luxurious carpeting beneath his feet.

"Very nice, guys," he said aloud.

Then he ambled to the window and gazed out over the city. Their room was high in one of the shiny, reflectorized curved spires that made the hotel such a landmark. A light, dingy blanket of smog lay over the City of Angels.

He had grown up here, near Glendale to be exact.

Now traffic was a royal pain in the ass. The city was running out of water. Like some massive, thirsty dragon, it had already pillaged Owens Lake some three hours to the north in the Sierra Nevada, and in a few years other sources would be gone as well. The smog was worse than ever.

And he loved it.

As far as he was concerned, the introduction to the old *Dragnet* TV show was right on: "This is the City," *the* city, as if there were no other.

Lyons had learned L.A.'s streets as a cop. There would be new streets now of course. And in the years that had passed some of the old familiar ones would be gone or changed. Moreover, he had seen a lot of other cities since his association with Stony Man Farm.

L.A. was still *the* city.

It was history in the making, vibrant and always in motion, the people living and dying like the cells of some vibrant organism.

He wondered if the Bonaventure was part of their mission somehow. Or had Schwarz and Blancanales just blown one by the old man, so to speak? It felt nice to put on the ritz once in a while, especially on the Stony Man tab.

He'd find out when they got here, and glancing at his watch, he thought that should be any minute.

By a quarter to four they still hadn't arrived. Lyons frowned; after all, they were supposed to make contact with Stony Man Farm at four.

Idly he turned on the TV set in the room.

Unlike the televisions in many of the motels he had stayed in, this one was new and had sharp, clear color. It also had a variety of pay TV channels, including some of the movie channels.

He flipped the dial and finally watched the last ten minutes of a rerun of *The Lucy Show*. Then it was four o'clock and time to make contact with home base.

Brognola came on the line immediately.

"Howdy, Chief. What's goin' on?"

"Carl! You all get there okay? Any problems?"

"The others aren't here."

"What?"

"I said, Gadgets and Politician aren't here. They haven't checked in yet."

Brognola's voice was suddenly all business, all pro. "Any reason to suspect anything irregular about that?"

"Negative. But then again, I don't really have a clue one way or the other."

"Let me check their flights," Brognola said. "Stand by, Ironman."

Lyons started to ask Brognola how he would check their flights, then thought better of it. Of course he knew how he would do it. Or, more accurately how the Bear would do it. Hell, that guy probably had better access to airline computers than most of the airlines themselves.

Waiting for Brognola, he flipped channels on the TV until he found a news station. Then he settled back on one of the beds, phone to his ear, and watched while he waited for Brognola to come back on the line.

The anchorwoman was attractive and blond. When she spoke, she gave the impression that she was speaking directly to him. Now that's what they call "presence," he thought.

"Police are investigating the bizarre capture of three bank robbers earlier this afternoon," she said.

Lyons watched with some interest. Any way to catch bank robbers was a good way, he thought. But, "bizarre"?

"We go now to reporter Jack Hanson, live at the scene."

The camera cut to a city street. Lyons could see the freeway in the background, the embankments sporting a profusion of ice plant. In the foreground, an old Dodge Charger was crashed against a telephone pole. Several LAPD black-and-white units were on the scene. Three men in handcuffs were being led to one of the units.

Lyons liked that. If there was anything that looked good on dirtbag bank robbers, it was handcuffs.

In the forefront of the whole scene, newsman Jack Hanson recounted the facts.

"It's a scene straight out of a James Bond thriller. Shortly after 2:00 p.m., three armed gunmen robbed the First Fidelity Bank of Los Angeles on Wilshire Boulevard. The trio fled in what witnesses described as an old Dodge Charger. The police pursued over several miles of surface streets at speeds in excess of eighty miles an hour. At one point it appeared that the suspects had successfully eluded the police. Then two officers following a likely path where the car might have fled got an early Christmas present.

"Behind me, you see the suspects' car where it was found crashed into a telephone pole. The suspects themselves were found *inside* the car, in the back seat, handcuffed with their hands behind their backs."

Lyons stared at the screen. For some reason the names of his two partners crossed his mind. The coincidence would be staggering, and yet, it just sort of had that smell somehow....

"The guns and the money were recovered in the trunk of the robbers' getaway car. The police are seeking two men, one of them described as a Latino male with a stocky build and the other an older male Caucasian, in connection with the mysterious apprehension of the robbers."

A broad grin spread over Lyons's face, a mixture of disbelief and glee. If his guess was correct, he couldn't wait to inform Gadgets of how he had been described as an "older male Caucasian."

Brognola came on the line. "Well, they made their flight from Seattle," he announced. "It didn't get in until a couple of hours or so ago. It seems likely they got caught in traffic."

"Hang on, Chief," interjected Lyons. "I may have the answer. There's something on the news that just may be it."

"The news?" Brognola's voice had a note of dread.

"Hang tight, boss," Lyons said. He listened intently to the reporter.

"Witnesses state that the fleeing robbers apparently tried to commandeer a vehicle driven by the two mystery men after their own car was wrecked. The two men, however, were heavily armed and captured the robbers. Then they locked the gunmen in their own car and fled the scene.

"Police are speculating that the men may have been undercover government or law-enforcement agents. One of the witnesses suggested the two men may possibly have been working for the CIA. Inquiries are being made, police say. Channel 18 will keep you up-to-date on any late-breaking developments in this bizarre episode."

Lyons lay back on the bed and howled with laughter. On the phone, Brognola's voice boomed in his ear.

"What is it, Carl? Did they get there? What's this about the news?"

The Ironman thought swiftly. No point in getting the Chief all worked up about it, not yet anyway. Especially after the big deal he had made about Lyons's offhand remark about the "search warrant" in San Diego.

Shit, the Chief had almost come unglued on that one. Lyons had only been referring to the joking label he and Gene-O had given to the cylinder head. Yet Brognola had given him the speech—not the abridged edition, but the long version, no less—about security and anonymity.

Besides, it would be fun to save this from the Chief. That way he could "pimp" on Gadgets and Politician, leading them to believe that Brognola knew and was real angry.

"Uh, nothing, really, Chief. News just says the traffic near the airport was at its worst today. All kinds of bizarre stuff happening. They probably just got held up by that."

"I see. All right, then."

"So, what's the mission about, boss?"

Brognola didn't answer that question. "How are you feeling these days, Carl?"

"I'm fine, Chief. But you didn't tell me about the mission. What's going down?"

"You feel pretty good, you say? In all respects? I mean, emotionally as well as physically?"

Lyons gave an exasperated frown at the anchorwoman and, with his free hand, pointed to the receiver he held against his ear as though sharing his frustration with her.

"Boss, how come you keep avoiding what I'm asking you? How come you keep answering my question with questions of your own?"

"Am I doing that?" Brognola said.

Exasperated, Lyons tossed the receiver up in the air and caught it on the way down. To the anchorwoman on the TV set, he asked, "How would you like to take this guy for a short walk, honey?"

She didn't show any visible enthusiasm at the suggestion, but kept right on reading the news.

Brognola's voice boomed in his ear. "Is there somebody in the room there with you?"

"Hang on a second, Chief."

"Carl! Need I remind you that it's a serious breach of security to call on this line if anybody else is in the room, except in the case of emergency? What the hell is the matter with you, anyway?"

Lyons came back on the line. "Sorry, Chief. I was just trying to get you a date with this newslady on the TV. Now, what were you saying about the mission?"

Brognola sighed. He sometimes wondered if he were maybe a little lax on the discipline—not to mention protocol—with his men. Still, when it was necessary, they shaped up immediately. And they would all lay their lives on the line whenever he asked them to; hell, they did it all the time. That was pretty good discipline, come to think of it.

It also took a certain rebellious, unbending streak for a man to be able to do what the members of Able Team did. You had to be a little crazy, in other words.

"Crazy." The word reminded Brognola of his initial concerns about Lyons, and whether or not he should send the Ironman on this mission, given the circumstances.

In a peculiar way, Carl's horseplay had reassured him a little. In Brognola's experience, the better Lyons felt about things in general, the more cocky he was.

Maybe he could handle it, after all.

"The mission's a go," he said. "But I want to have all of you there for the briefing. Let's make contact at, oh, say eleven tomorrow morning, your time. Yes, call here at 1100 hours, L.A. time."

"Roger, Chief."

"The rooms okay?" Brognola inquired as an after-thought.

Lyons was instantly wary. "Uh, just great, Chief. No problems at all, really. About what you'd expect, I guess."

"Clean, quiet, that sort of thing?"

"Absolutely, Chief. No problems at all."

Brognola seemed satisfied at that, and Lyons didn't want to press the issue until he had talked to Gadgets and Blancanales. Finally Brognola, who sounded to Lyons as if he had made up his mind about something, spoke again.

"Very well, then," he said crisply. "Make contact at eleven."

11

Carl Lyons was the first to get up. He opened his eyes and, for a moment, wondered if it were still night. Then he realized what caused the sensation. Heavy, light-blocking curtains were located behind the regular drapes, making the room dark even when the sun was up.

A little slowly, a little stiffly, he pulled himself out of bed. He found a pair of gym shorts and his running shoes and went out.

He did a leisurely half hour, running at a pace he estimated as eight- or nine-minute miles, an easy stride to clear the mind as well as the body. Then, on his return to the hotel, he found the pool and decided to do a few fast laps.

He also found Gadgets.

His partner was already in the pool, doing slow laps with a crawl stroke that looked completely effortless and lazy. Lyons knew that if it looked that easy, it meant the swimming was efficient and the result of long practice.

At the end of one of the laps, Gadgets saw him and stopped.

"Yo, Ironman," he hailed.

"Don't stop on my account," Lyons replied. "That looks real good for an 'older male Caucasian.'"

"Fuck off," his partner replied good-naturedly, and went back to his crawl.

Lyons jumped in and did a few fast laps, then clambered out and sat on the edge of the pool. His legs dangled in the water, cooling and relaxing his calves, which still felt tight from the run. Then, when Gadgets finished his laps, the two men returned to Blancanales's room.

Politician was still asleep. He woke quickly and unpleasantly when Lyons's wet towel hit him in the face.

"I've killed people for less than that," he said, not entirely jokingly.

"You may get your chance," Lyons responded.

The Ironman felt good, felt great, in fact. The blues of the past few days—and of the distant past—were gone. He had buried them, along with the regrets and the bodies of those whose ship had stopped. Time to get on with living.

Blancanales finished a quick shower and shave, and the three men went for breakfast in the restaurant of the hotel.

Like the room, the food was excellent. Some thirty dollars later, they stepped off the elevator back onto their floor.

"Damn, it's great to be alive," Lyons exclaimed as they walked down the hallway toward their rooms.

Schwarz grimaced at Blancanales, the latter nursing a mild hangover. "Spare us the 'high on life bullshit,' amigo," Politician said. "I think I like you better when you're a morose bastard, walking around in a cloud of gloom. At least then you're not so obnoxiously cheerful."

Lyons grinned.

He glanced at his watch—10:52 a.m. Just perfect, he thought. They arrived at the door to his room, and Lyons opened it, standing to one side of the doorframe as he had been trained to do ever since he'd been a rookie patrolman answering his first call on the LAPD.

Zip-zip-zip-zip-zip!

"Shit!"

Even as he spat out the oath, Lyons saw the man inside.

He could also see the blunt end of the silencer on the muzzle of the automatic weapon in the man's hands. The "zips" were the hot little 9 mm bullets screaming past him, followed by the louder smacking as the bullets hit the wall on the far side of the corridor.

Ambush!

In a single, lightning-fast motion, the Ironman drew back behind the safety of the doorframe, crouched and came out again, down low, where an ambusher might not expect such a quick response. The .45 Government Model fit snugly in his hand.

The doorknob was on the left side of this particular door as he faced it from the outside. Lyons had stood to the far left of it, beyond the doorframe when he'd inserted the key, turned the knob and pushed the door open.

The precaution had saved his life.

It wasn't that the Ironman had been expecting trouble. In fact quite the opposite was true. But ever since he'd seen a training film on structure approach while in the LAPD academy, Lyons approached every house and every apartment in the same manner.

Even the houses of the girls he dated.

"There's another reason for that, men," the training officer had told them at the police academy. "Especially if it's a blind date. You know, when somebody who used to be your best buddy is supposedly doing you a favor, setting you up with her."

"Sir, what's that, sir?" one of the recruits had asked.

"If she's real ugly, you can run off to the side, dodge between the next house and be gone. She'll never get a look at your face, or be able to identify you later."

But the actual incident on the film had been nothing like that. Instead, it had been a grim reminder of the cost of not following a few basic safety precautions.

The film was a reenactment of the slaying of a Los Angeles patrolman. The officer in the film responded to a routine disturbance call and walked up to the front door to ring the doorbell.

Afterward, the investigators pieced it all together. The disturbance was caused by a distraught and suicidal man inside. He was waving a shotgun around, threatening to kill his wife and then himself. She finally tried to wrestle it from his grip, and the two were struggling over it when the officer knocked.

With the strength of paranoid rage, the man wrenched the shotgun free, turned and fired instantly. It was an old double-barrel twelve-gauge loaded with number three shot.

Lyons had pictured the result even more vividly than the training film had depicted. Number three wasn't buckshot, he knew, but it wasn't the fine stuff you used for doves, either. The officer took both blasts in the chest and was DOA.

There was another lesson in that incident as well. Nothing is "routine" in police business.

The same thing held true for Stony Man business, only more so.

As he came out around the doorframe, down low, about two feet off the ground, Lyons's eyesight found the man. He was straight ahead, dressed in street clothing, holding an Uzi at his side, ready to spray more 9 mm destruction at the doorway.

It all seemed to happen in slow motion.

Lyons's brain sent the message to pull the trigger on the .45 Government Model.

Once, twice, a third time.

Three should do it, he thought, all the time being aware that there may be more men in the room, or that he may have to put one or two more in the first one.

At the same instant, his eyes transmitted the sensory data on the man's location. The brain processed it and gave the signals to his right hand to make the necessary aiming adjustments, shifting the gun muzzle to the left and up a little. Simultaneously the grip tightened to pull the trigger, all in the flash of a microsecond....

Then, in the same instant, the ambusher's eyes widened as his own gaze saw Lyons, down low.

The gunman was all pro, the Ironman noted. The killer had two options, try for cover or adjust his own aim to the new, lower threat. In an untrained man or an amateur, the survival instinct usually won out, and the decision would have been to dive behind the wall in the room. Or try to, anyway.

This guy didn't.

He stayed to fight, using the same microsecond of time to attack, not retreat. He did this even though his own brain probably realized that Lyons had a quarter-second "initiator's advantage," and if Lyons was any good at all it was probably all over for him.

Moving at the speed of light, the nerve signals reached Lyons's hand.

Boom! Boom! Boom!

The three blasts from the Government Model, each punctuated by the sharp click-clack of the slide, seemed deafening in the confined room. The gunman staggered backward as the heavy slugs hammered his torso, then Lyons was scuttling forward into the room, gun ready, diving ahead to press his slim advantage in case the man had a backup.

Chasing your bullets, they called it.

The danger zone, he knew, would be the main body of the bedroom, which opened off to the left ahead of him. The gunman could easily have a partner behind the wall, another ambusher with a silenced 9 mm automatic weapon.

Every fiber in his body tight and quick, every nerve alive, the Ironman streaked ahead. The .45 might as well have been part of his own body, a lethal extension of death. He felt wonderfully, completely alive, filled with the rush of making a dangerous gamble he thought he would win.

The gunman's body was still staggering backward, propelled by the impact of three slugs in the chest.

Going low, Lyons flashed into the main area of the room. Just as quickly, his eyes registered that it was empty, except for the beds, the furniture, the clothing.

Lyons had moved so fast that the killer was still on his feet. He had staggered backward into the far wall. Now he was half stepping, half falling forward, the brain dead and the body just beginning to get the message.

As a gesture of bravado and a celebration of having won, Lyons let his own charge continue even after he saw there was no threat left in the room. Then, at the last instant, he turned his left shoulder into the gunman's slumping form.

"Uuhh!"

It was a dead man's groan.

Lyons's maneuver made a hard, solid body block that slammed the dead man backward into the wall. The impact drove the sound out of the dead killer's throat, a process that was nothing more than the mechanics of air being driven from the lungs through the larynx. Lyons spun the other way and once again scanned the room behind him, making sure his initial sight had been accurate.

It was.

No backup anywhere. Just one man with a silenced automatic assault weapon.

Behind him, Lyons was aware of his partners. Pros that they were, Blancanales and Schwarz had each drawn their guns. When Lyons had fired and then followed his rounds into the room, Blancanales had taken his place on the left side of the door. Unlike Lyons, however, he stood, so that if he had to shoot, he wouldn't be on the same level as the low-moving Ironman.

Gadgets, meanwhile, had run across the open doorway and taken up a similar position to the right of the door.

In the single second after Lyons had entered the room, it had become obvious there was only one threat, and that he had neutralized it.

Blancanales stepped swiftly inside the room, his back to the wall, to provide better cover in case some other enemy should belatedly appear. In the hallway, Gadgets checked the wall on the far side opposite the door.

A wallpaper with a busy pattern covered the wall. The five holes from the 9 mm made an irregular circular pattern at low-chest level. Good aiming, Gadgets thought. Still, the holes weren't too visible, though in two of them a shred of wallpaper stuck out, perhaps caused by the bullets losing stability in flight and tumbling or "keyholing" as they entered.

Strange, Gadgets thought, a 9 mm usually wouldn't do that. Maybe the silencer had thrown off the flight a little.

He stepped over and pressed down the shreds of wallpaper, thumbing them against the wall so that they were less visible. Then, swiftly, he stooped and picked up the three brass cartridges from Lyons's .45. Two of them were close by; the third had bounced an uncharacteristically long distance away.

Then he, too, ducked inside the room and closed the doorway gently behind him.

THE WESTIN BONAVENTURE looked as if it had been built to last. Its walls were strong, solid, well insulated, all of which were helpful and reassuring in the face of Southern California's known propensity for earthquakes.

It also meant the 9 mm slugs didn't go clear through the wall where they struck, opposite the room occupied by Carl Lyons.

They did, however, get the attention of the guest in the room opposite that wall.

Bill Johnston, regional vice president of sales for a company that produced quality cookies, cakes and breads, occupied that room. When the incident had begun, he'd been sitting in one of the hotel's comfortable chairs, studying sales figures for his company. Johnston, a shrewd and careful analyst, had been sifting through them, trying to discern trends to make predictions.

What he'd heard was a brief hammering on the wall, as if someone were driving a nail to hang a picture. Hard on the heels of that, he'd heard a couple of muffled booms.

Now Johnston was frowning.

The hammering he didn't mind, but the booms didn't sound quite right.

He considered it for a moment, then shrugged and got to his feet. A distinguished man in his late forties, Johnston wasn't the type of man who looked the other way to avoid "getting involved." It was probably nothing, but he had to check.

Bill opened the door and gazed down the hallway.

Nothing.

Nobody there, nothing out of place.

He wrinkled his brow, looking, thinking. A faint, acrid odor hung in the air. It seemed vaguely familiar, something he had smelled before, but he couldn't remember where.

Oh, well, he thought. Probably some drunk conventioneers or business people banging on the wall. Pretty early in the day to get drunk, though. Still, you never know what people will do when they're out of town.

Johnston knew those types.

Some guys spend so much time partying when they go out of town on business that they aren't worth a damn at taking care of business. He didn't mind that, as long as they were on the other side, and not his.

He withdrew into his room and shut the door. Then he remembered where he had smelled that smell.

It was like gunpowder, in a way. Or maybe caps from a cap gun. Or the smell that those party favors make, the little gizmos that you hold tightly in one hand and pull the attached string with the other. When you did, it made one hell of a loud bang and shot streamers into the air.

Yeah, that was what it smelled like.

Goddamn conventioneers, he thought.

12

"Friend of yours?"

Gadgets winked as he asked the question. He had just closed the door to the hotel room. Now he folded his arms across his chest and surveyed the room and the other three men, one of whom didn't work anymore.

"Not me," Lyons said, grinning.

"Me, neither," agreed Politician.

Gadgets sighed. "You know, the crime rate in this city is flat getting out of hand. To think things would get to the point where a guy can't even visit his hometown without some dude breaking into his room and getting all hostile with a gun."

"Criminal justice system sucks," agreed Lyons. "But then, it's been that way for years."

The Ironman felt good. Something *was* definitely up, he thought. They had a mission, all right, even if the Chief hadn't yet seen fit to tell them about it. Moreover, even at the risk of vanity, he had to admit he was pleased at the way he had responded to the ambush. The old reflexes were still there.

He regarded the dead man on the floor.

The intruder lay on his back, arms outflung from the impact of Lyons's body block. The legs were slightly apart, one knee bent, the other leg straight. His mouth was slightly open, his eyes gazing sightlessly at whatever or into wherever dead guys' eyes look. He was medium-sized, stocky, with very white, untanned skin.

"Well," Lyons said at last, "what do you say we get this rude asshole out of here?"

"What do you have in mind, amigo?" inquired Politician. "Open the window and give a 'yo-heave-ho,' or just put him out in the hallway? Or maybe call the front desk and ask them to store him for us?"

"None of those. Let's just chuck him in the bathtub for now."

"Why?"

"Why not? Get him out of our sight, for one thing. For another, this is a damn nice room, and it's a shame to have him shedding his blood all over the carpet."

"His *Russian* blood, you mean."

Gadgets spoke quietly. He had moved over and was squatting down on his haunches, studying the dead man's features carefully.

"What do you mean?" asked Lyons.

"Well, it's nothing I can be sure of, but I'd bet lunch that this guy is from Eastern Europe somewhere."

"How so?"

"Look." Gadgets pointed at the man's face. "Looks Slavic to me. And look at the skin tone. It's got that grainy, dead-fish pallor one associates with that part of the world."

"Maybe that's because he *is* a dead fish," Lyons said, grinning. "And he's probably well on the way to being bloodless, too."

He tucked the .45 into his belt and bent down to grip the man's arms. Blancanales grabbed the feet, and together they carried their limp burden into the bathroom. Fortunately most of the bleeding appeared to be internal; none of the rounds had exited—"no through-and-through 'ers," as

Lyons put it—and the blood hadn't flowed with any real vigor from the entrance wounds.

When they got the dead man into the bathroom, they perched him on the edge of the tub. Gadgets searched his clothing for a wallet or any other form of identification. It was no easy task, because the dead man's limp form kept trying to loll one way and then the other.

Nothing. No form of ID.

"Well, that's hardly surprising," said Lyons grimly. "I guess we can't really expect him to carry a photo ID from 'Assassins International,' or some similar organization."

"That's true enough," agreed Gadgets. "Be nice if they would, though."

Lyons let go of the man's body, giving it a slight push backward as he did so. The corpse thumped heavily into the tub. The head hit the tiled wall with a bony crack. Then the body seemed to settle into the tub, crossway with a sort of reluctant resignation, the back of the knees still hooked over the edge.

Gadgets was right, Lyons thought.

The guy looks Russian as hell. The dead eyes seemed to gaze balefully at him. Lyons imagined he could read a sort of cruelty in the man's face, that Soviet indifference to the suffering of others. Or perhaps that wasn't quite accurate, he amended. That indifference probably didn't originate with the people who lived in the Soviet Union, but with the Soviet political machine.

Either way this guy had it.

"We will bury you," Nikita Khrushchev had said. When was that? Late fifties? Early sixties? When Eisenhower or Kennedy, one of them, was president, Lyons thought. Whenever Khrushchev was premier, anyway.

And the Russians meant it, Lyons knew. At least they were going to give it one hell of a try.

Well, asshole, maybe you will bury us. And then again, maybe you won't, Lyons thought grimly. Death is pretty fucking indifferent, too, and the Russians end up just as dead as the rest of us. They just cause a lot of terror and misery along the way.

The Ironman regarded the corpse for a few more moments. Then suddenly he grimaced.

"Looks sloppy," he commented out loud to nobody in particular. He lifted the dead man's legs and swung them into the tub. Then he jerked the shower curtain closed.

"RIP, asshole."

The thrill of victory—of surviving, actually—and the adrenaline rush of combat had faded. In their place, Lyons was starting to feel edgy and irritable, a sort of postcombat letdown that was part physical, part mental.

He strode out of the bathroom.

Blancanales stood by the window, gazing out over the city. Schwarz wasn't in the room.

"Where's—"

The Ironman's inquiry was cut short by the room's door opening. Then Gadgets was there, holding several cans of fruit juice from the vending machine down the hall. Wordlessly he tossed one to each of his partners. Then he opened a third for himself.

Lyons drained the orange juice in a single long pull, then he stepped to the phone and dialed the number for Stony Man Farm. His watch read 11:14 a.m.

"You're late," Brognola boomed this observation in a matter-of-fact rather than critical manner.

"Sorry, Chief."

"Everything all right? Blancanales and Schwarz finally show up okay?"

"Affirmative on both counts."

After a moment's hesitation, Brognola went on crisply. "I've got a little project for you."

"We thought you might."

"Here's the story." Brognola paused. "Say, I don't suppose there are any extension phones in that room, are there?"

"Negative, Chief. Why? You worried about security?"

"No. Nothing like that. I just wondered if there was some way the others could hear this. No matter. You can fill them in on the details, I suppose."

Lyons winked at his two friends, who of course could hear every booming word Brognola said. "No problem, boss. I'll see they get the message all right."

"Fine. Now here's what we've got."

The Stony Man chief proceeded to run down the facts. He described seven instances where the marauders had hit and run. Each time it had been at a home in a wealthy but not superrich area. Each time there had been no attempt at subtlety, nor had they even waited until the homeowners had gone out.

"And there may be more than that," Brognola added. "Maybe as many as sixteen over the past year."

"How so?"

"The FBI has put a team of MO specialists on it. Our friends in the Bureau have pulled police reports from all over the country. In some cases, the reports aren't sufficiently detailed to make a positive determination that the same gang was responsible."

"That's pretty sloppy police work," Lyons muttered. "Especially considering how distinctive these guys sound."

"What? Oh, yes. It is. Be that as it may, that's basically what we've got."

"Any other information on these guys?" Lyons questioned.

Lyons could hear the rustle of papers two thousand miles away as Brognola scanned the file before him. The head Fed told Lyons what he had.

Typically four men were involved. Heavily armed. Dressed in camou fatigues. Carried out the attacks with military precision. Two of the assaults reported six attackers; one said there were only three.

"Descriptions?" Lyons inquired.

"Sure. Their faces were green and brown and black. That's helpful, isn't it?"

"Shouldn't be too hard to spot," agreed Lyons with a wink to his partners. "Can't be that many guys who look like that, either. But just to be on the compulsive side, are there any other details about what they look like?"

Brognola read them off. "Two of the men were big. One of the big ones had large muscles and a beard, sort of a pro football lineman type. The other one was huge but not muscular, just huge. Oh, yes, this other one has an eight tattoed on the top of his head. Otherwise he's bald."

"A nate?" Lyons was puzzled. "What's a nate, Chief?"

"Not 'a nate,' Ironman. I said 'an eight.' You know, the number, eight."

"An eight on his pate," whispered Gadgets to Blancanales. Politician rolled his eyes in mock disgust.

"Oh." Lyons understood now. "What about the others?"

"One is real skinny. But wiry. Muscular. Several of the witnesses have said he's got weird eyes. Scary—like Charles Manson."

"And the other one?"

"Nothing really remarkable about him. Just an ordinary-looking guy apparently. At least he's the one nobody seems to remember much about."

Lyons thought it over. Then Gadgets got his attention. "Ask him about the others," he whispered.

"What others?"

"Didn't he say some of the cases said there were six? What did the others look like?"

Lyons repeated the question.

"Let's see now," Brognola muttered, more to himself than to Lyons. "Hang on." Lyons heard papers rustle, then the Chief came back on the line. "Not too much, I'm afraid. In both cases it appears that one of the other two men was real big. The other was normal . . . umm."

Lyons shrugged at Gadgets as they waited.

"Hello." Brognola's voice had taken on a tone of sudden insight, a recognition of something significant.

"What is it, Chief?"

"In both cases one of the additional suspects was big. Muscular, like the lineman guy with the beard who's been in all the robberies. In fact, one of the witnesses said these two looked so similar they could be brothers. Big, hairy bastards. This extra guy has tattoos, though. Snakes, it looks like, tangled snakes on his arms."

Something in that description stirred Lyons's memory.

Mentally he reached for it, groping for the significance. It eluded him, however, and flitted away down the corridors of his mind. Instead of forcing it he backed off. No sweat, he thought, it'll come.

"What about the other guy?"

"Looked normal. Not much help there."

Lyons looked at Gadgets, who shrugged. A long pause followed, which Lyons finally broke.

"So what are the orders, Chief?"

"I want you to go after them."

"And . . . ?"

"What do you mean?" Brognola asked in exasperation.

Lyons grinned. He was feeling great again, a hundred and ten percent, as his football coach used to say. This was an old game between him and Brognola, making his chief come out and say what he wanted done even though he already knew.

It went back to Lyons's days as a cop. A fond fantasy of the officers who worked the worst inner-city beats was to hear orders like that. They used to imagine having a lieutenant at the preshift lineup read a directive in that vein from the briefing bulletin.

"One other thing, you guys," the lieutenant would say. "In view of the serious overcrowding of the jail population, we're not going to be making arrests on major felonies. You get that? Hey, listen up, Lyons, Dressler, Strumsky, all you guys, shut up. You, too, Criss. Roberts. Albini. No arrests on violent felonies. Just waste 'em. Shoot the bastards. Yeah, you heard me right. Comes from the commissioner to the chief to me to you. Everybody got it?"

"Question, Lieutenant?" he would ask.

"Yeah, Lyons."

"What paper do we write on it? An incident report, a one-five-three, or what?"

"Hmmm. Good question. Ah, to hell with it. Just advise dispatch whenever you ice somebody, make a log entry and then go back in service."

Of course it never happened. Probably just as well, too, Lyons thought in hindsight. There were so many deserving assholes on the street that it would be an impossible task. Easier to just let the courts keep muddling along.

Still, it was pleasant to imagine. It was also fun to put Brognola on the spot at times like this.

"Well, Chief?"

"You know what I'm telling you, Ironman, but if it will satisfy your childish whims, I'll say it. Kill them."

"Thank you. How?"

"How?" Brognola exploded. "What the hell do you mean? However you want, that's how. Shoot 'em, stab 'em, blow 'em up, starve them to fucking death if you like. Whatever suits your karma. Whatever way makes you feel like a fulfilled human being. Shit, Lyons!"

The Ironman grinned at his partners. Usually he didn't get to Brognola that way.

"What I mean, Chief," he continued patiently, "is this. How do we find them? Do you have an itinerary of their targets, so we just wait for the next one that's conveniently nearby? Or do we just guess at where they'll hit next? You got an informant on them, or what?"

Brognola was silent. Finally he spoke. "All right, Lyons. You got me on that one. A fair question, I suppose."

"Do you have a plan of some sort?"

"As a matter of fact, Ironman, I do."

"So tell me."

"In due time. There's a lot of background info here that has a bearing on how we're going to do it. And when. And for that matter, why."

It seemed that when the marauders hit a house in L.A. the lady who lived there had gotten a real good look at the assailants. She had also gotten away, causing the robbery to be aborted, but that wasn't the main point.

The main point was that a few days later she happened to recognize two of the guys on television.

It was a one-in-a-million fluke, a coincidence of staggering proportions. A local news reporter had been doing a story on roving checkpoints used by the border patrol on remote stretches of the southwest. And who should drive through the checkpoint but the attackers....

The checkpoints were one of many efforts by the border patrol to halt the tide of Mexican nationals who entered the U.S. to work.

The problem was out of control—many of the aliens went back and forth across the border virtually at will. The border patrol, hopelessly undermanned and without the total support of Washington politicians, set up random roadblocks on deserted stretches of highway. It had become commonplace to apprehend the aliens by the carful.

A news station on a slow day had sent a crew out to one of the checkpoints. The camera crew shot footage of fifteen cars and trucks passing through the point. Fourteen were legit; the fifteenth contained illegal aliens.

The fourth vehicle, however, was a van that contained four men, apparently going on a hunting trip.

By sheerest chance, the female victim at the last assault had seen the newscast and had called the police.

"What happened?" asked Lyons, intrigued.

"She called the cops, who at first thought she was some nut, of course. Then the cops called the border patrol, and the sheriff's department in the county where the checkpoint was."

"And?"

"Well, by then, the suspects were long gone. But the camera footage is there. They made some stills of the face shots, and flyers have been sent out to every law-enforcement agency in the country."

Lyons thought it over. "I still don't see how we're going to go after them, even if we have pictures of some of them."

"You're not. You're going fishing," Brognola replied.

"Oh?"

"Yes. You're not after them."

"Oh."

"You see, Carl, *they* are going to come after you."

13

"What a sweetheart," Lyons observed when Brognola finished describing the situation and his plan for handling it.

"Isn't he, though?" agreed the Stony Man Operations chief.

The Ironman's comment wasn't directed at the plan itself, but at the leader of the gang.

This guy, it seemed, had developed some kind of fixation on the woman who had recognized him. He deliberately harassed both the woman and her husband, a scientist of some kind, Lyons gathered.

"We're talking more than just intimidating a witness, Carl," Brognola had explained.

Old anger surged up in Lyons.

It went back to his years as a cop. He had learned only too well in those days that witness intimidation by the criminals worked. It worked well. It was s.o.p.—standard operating procedure—for organized crime of all types, from the traditional Mafia to such nontraditional groups as outlaw motorcycle gangs, drug dealers and Asian gangs such as the yakuza.

Other crooks had been quick to recognize the benefits of such tactics. And, impotent as the courts were at addressing the problem, it had become commonplace in nonorganized crime settings as well. Even in "routine" murders and assaults, the victim or witnesses were liable to get the message.

He'd seen it work time and again.

It took various forms, but the effect was always the same. The telephone would ring in the middle of the night. "Drop the charges. Don't go to the cops. Don't tell shit to the cops," someone would say on the phone.

When the victim angrily protested, an incentive would be provided. Sometimes the witness would be personally threatened. Sometimes the demand would be preceded or followed by a mysterious "drive-by shooting" of his house or apartment.

Sometimes the approach would be more subtle.

"Your son, Johnnie," someone would whisper over the phone. "Third-grader, isn't he? Blond hair? Likes to wear that Dodgers baseball cap? Mrs. Andrews's class? Gets out at two-thirty, doesn't he? Unless something's happened to him in the meantime...."

Lyons remembered one case where the witness came home to find that the family pet, a cat, had been decapitated and the head nailed to the front door of the house.

Almost invariably, when a witness "rolled over" or changed testimony in a case, it was because of such tactics. He'd seen it happen—even with witnesses who were on the stand under oath.

"Didn't you tell the police it was this man who fired the gun?" the prosecutor would ask.

"I don't remember," the witness would say.

"Would it help refresh your recollection if I showed you your own handwritten statement?"

"No. If I said that, I was wrong."

"Sir, are you aware of the penalties for perjury?"

And the poor bastard on the witness stand would stare ahead in stony silence. Even the "good citizen" witnesses clammed up, because what they could not say was that the court's penalty for perjury was one hell of a lot better than the crooks' penalty for telling the truth. It was a classic example of being between a rock and a hard place. The case would go down the tubes, and the credibility of the cops and "the system" would take yet another nosedive.

The Ironman's voice was tight with anger when he responded to Brognola's comment. "'Just intimidating a witness,' as you put it, is bad enough in my book, Chief."

"I'm not arguing with you on that," Brognola said. "All I'm saying is that this case involved intimidation, and a lot more besides."

"Tell me about this fixation, then."

"Guy refers to her as 'Sara.' Keeps calling her that like he thinks it's her name."

"It's not her name, I take it."

"Absolutely not. At any rate, since the raid, there have been several attempts on her life—on all their lives, actually—including threats made to the kids. A campaign of terror, actually."

"Maybe he thinks that her name is actually Sara."

"We considered that," responded Brognola. "But it seems unlikely. Her true name was printed in the paper when the robbery happened. And again on the news when she broke the case, so to speak. Also..."

"What, Chief?" Lyons urged.

"The victim—this woman—says that while the robbery was going on the guy was looking at her real strangely. Called her 'Sara' then and said some weird stuff to her."

"What kind of weird stuff?"

"I don't have all the details here. But the FBI put a shrink on it, and he concluded that this guy had some psychiatric disorder that was triggered by that name."

From the bed, Gadgets mouthed the question, "What kind of disorder? Some sort of sexual fixation?"

Lyons repeated the question.

From the other end of the line came Brognola's sigh and the sound of papers rustling. "Hang on. I saw it here somewhere. Oh, yes, here it is. Something about paranoid schizophrenia...let's see," he muttered. "Disassociative state...repression of childhood trauma...transference—hell, I can't make any sense out of this stuff."

Lyons had heard enough. "Sounds like the guy's a fucking wacko. That's all we need to know for now."

"Agreed," said Brognola. "Since then there have been two attempts on her life. One was a letter bomb. The other was made to look like a traffic accident."

"What happened?"

"Why didn't they work, you mean? Well, the letter bomb simply malfunctioned. A dud round, so to speak. This lady gets a package. It's addressed in handwriting that she thinks she recognizes. She opens it and finds herself looking at the guts of a bomb and enough plastic explosive to level their house."

Lyons let out a low whistle. "These guys play hardball."

"They're well organized," Brognola agreed.

"And the traffic accident?"

Brognola's voice was quiet. "It worked. Only they got the wrong car. Woman and her kid killed, fried. Completely innocent."

Lyons was quiet for several moments. Finally he spoke. "Anything else to this case, Chief? Any international overtones, so to speak?"

"What do you mean? Why do you ask that?" Brognola's voice was casual, completely offhand. It was so much so, in fact, that Lyons, who knew him well, could tell he was covering something up when he said it.

"See, there's this guy in our bathtub. Gadgets, who's not exactly a dummy on these matters, seems to think he's a Ruski."

"What's he doing in your bathtub, Carl?"

"Bleeding."

"Bleeding? Is he still alive?"

"Does a guy have to be alive to bleed? I'd say that actually what we have is blood leaking out of him by the force of gravity."

"What's it leaking out through? As if I didn't already have a pretty good idea."

"Three holes, each about forty-five hundredths across."

"I see." Brognola was silent for a moment. "And the three holes? I suppose you, uh—"

"Installed them? Ten-four. Did it myself, though my two partners were ready, willing and able to do it. As luck would have it, though, I was the guy to open the door, so I got to have all the fun."

"He was in your room?"

"That's affirmative."

On the other end of the line, Brognola sighed. "Things are moving faster than I thought," he mused. "This definitely adds a new dimension to the problem."

"Do tell," said Lyons in a dry voice. "Do tell."

They waited while Brognola thought. When he finally spoke, his voice sounded weary.

"We knew these guys had been in touch with the Russians," he said at last.

Lyons was aware that Gadgets and Blancanales had come to full alert on that one. The Ironman's incredulous voice mirrored his partners' interest. "The Russians, Chief? The Russians? What the hell are the Russians involved with these lowlifes for?"

Brognola explained about the stolen specifications for the national defense system, concluding with the point that while the papers weren't exactly the complete scale-model plans, they would certainly generate interest in the Soviet Union.

"Apparently," the Stony Man Operations chief said, "the thieves somehow figured out what they had. Or at least that it was top-secret stuff. As I said, we learned that they've been in touch with the Russians."

"How did we learn that?"

"It's a long story, and you don't have a need to know all the details. But in a nutshell, we have a sister agency working on the case. Their sources confirm that these marauders, these terrorists, are indeed trying to sell the stuff to the Russians."

"I see."

"They've also been trying to sell them back to us." Brognola's voice was hard. "Negotiations have been taking place for a couple of days."

"Why, Chief? Why haven't you gotten a fix on where they are. Then you could call in an air strike, as my friend Blancanales would put it?"

"Can't locate them. And they tell us they have other copies of the material placed with other sources who will give them to the Communists if we get cute."

"The highest bidder," Lyons observed.

"Precisely."

"And the leader's got a psycho fixation on this woman, besides. What a beaut!"

There was a pause in the conversation, then Brognola said, "However, as I said, we have a plan."

The plan seemed simple enough.

Brognola had called it "going fishing," and the term proved to be fairly appropriate. In fact, it was appropriate as hell. The only drawback was that to go fishing one needed bait.

"So what's the bait, Chief?"

"You are."

"Us?"

"Precisely. Able Team. And . . ." Brognola hesitated.

"And what, Chief?"

"And your ex-wife, Carl. Jane Odom."

For a moment Lyons's mind simply didn't accept the data. It didn't compute. Input error. Then it hit him.

"Janie?" The Ironman's voice was hoarse, stunned. "What's Janie have to do with this."

"She's married to the scientist." Brognola drew a deep breath. "She's . . . Sara."

14

Lyon's mind whirled, rocked by the impact of Brognola's revelation. Everywhere he turned it seemed the past was being flung in his face.

"Janie?" he repeated. "Are you sure?"

"I'm sure, Carl. She's Jane Odom now."

"I know that," Lyons said. "She's remarried, and she's happy, and I'm happy she's happy."

"Her husband is the scientist who had the papers that were taken by these terrorists," Brognola continued smoothly. "She's also the one who this guy thinks is 'Sara.'"

"And you want me—us, rather, but including me—to do this one?"

"That's why I'm talking to you."

"Jesus, sweet Jesus!" Lyons breathed. "You don't want too much, do you, boss?"

"If you don't want to take it on, all you have to do is say so." Brognola's voice had taken on an ice-cold, ice-hard edge. "I'm sure I could find another operative to do it."

"So why didn't you? Why are you coming to us first?"

"Simple. Two reasons, actually. One is that your ex, Jane, actually wrote you, asking for your help."

Lyons was stunned. "She did?"

"Yes. She makes it clear what the terms are of course. That her husband knows and agrees, for one. That you don't have to do it, for another." Brognola hesitated. "In my book, the fact she wrote gives you the right of first refusal for the mission, so to speak."

"What the hell do you mean by that?"

Brognola's voice showed he was losing his patience. "If I used somebody else, and it turned to shit and everybody got killed, you'd be mad as hell. Am I right, Carl? Especially when you found out that she'd asked for your help. This way, you get to have the choice."

"Some choice," Lyons muttered as he considered the facts. Once again he reminded himself that while Brognola was all hearty geniality on the outside he could be one cold, calculating bastard on the inside. Of course, at least he was good at it, a master tactician. And it was comforting to know that the guy who was calling the shots was, in fact, a tough son of a bitch.

"Read me the letter, Chief."

Brognola did. Lyons considered the words. "Nice little dig at the end, wouldn't you say?" he observed at last.

"What do you mean?"

"That bit about Tommy being like his biological father. That suggests I haven't been much more than that, never mind how long I lived like a stray dog while I tried to support them."

Brognola didn't respond.

Lyons let out a sigh. "But that's all history, isn't it? And who knows, maybe it's true." The questions were directed more to himself than to Brognola. "And for some strange reason, it doesn't matter anymore."

"What do you mean, Carl?"

"I mean, we all do what we think we have to do at the time. And today it's all as stale as yesterday's news." The Ironman still spoke as if distracted, thinking out loud. "You let it go, I guess, all the anger and the hurt and the guilt."

"Yes, I guess so." Brognola's voice sounded soft, as if embarrassed by this intimate glimpse into the feelings of such a tough man.

Lyons spoke again. This time his voice was clear and firm. "You said two reasons, Chief. What's the other?"

"Simple. You're the best team for the job."

Lyons grinned. If words were weapons, and debating was using them, Brognola was the toughest man alive.

"Well, Ironman?"

"Well, what?"

"Are you in or out?"

"I'm in."

"You're sure?"

"I said I'm in." Lyon's voice was strong, definitive.

"Good. Now here's what we're going to do."

From the efficient way the Chief had proceeded to outline the tactics, Lyons realized that Brognola had known all along what his response would be. Bastard just wanted *me* to say it, he thought. That way I couldn't squawk. Then, too, maybe it's a little payback for me making him spell out that he wanted us to ice the guys.

What a bastard, Lyons thought again. Then a faint smile traced his lips. But a tough one, all right.

Lyons felt very good indeed. The past was yesterday's news. And Lyons knew he was free of it as he returned his attention to Brognola's plan.

"The marauders wanted ten million dollars for the documents. The last offer by the U.S. was four," Brognola told them.

"Gee, is that all?" Lyons asked.

"As a matter of fact, it isn't," said Brognola. "The terrorists also want complete immunity from prosecution for all past crimes they may have committed. And the leader wants 'Sara.'"

"Question, Chief."

"Shoot."

"Why don't we just tell them to stick it up their asses?"

"Because we're stalling, of course." Brognola's voice was matter-of-fact.

"Oh."

"Yes. Now here's the plan. We give them what they want."

Lyons paused, his brow furrowed into deep creases. "We give them what they want? What the hell kind of plan is that? I want to kill these bastards, not play monopoly with them."

"Precisely. That's the idea."

"How so, Chief?"

"We agree to meet the leader. We agree to give him four million dollars. We agree to immunity. And we agree to give him 'Sara.' He, in turn, will give us the plans."

"Gee, boss. We're really driving a hard bargain, aren't we?" observed Lyons sarcastically. "Really yanking him around, aren't you?"

"Well, as a matter of fact, I have yanked him around, a good deal in fact. I'm giving you the bottom line of several hours of negotiating. And now he thinks I have reluctantly given in to this, which is a lot less than he wanted at first."

"So what happens when he shows up? Then we kill him?"

Brognola was unperturbed. "Precisely. When the marauders show up, we take them out. That is, you take them out. You and Politician and Gadgets."

"Just like that?"

"Just like that."

There was one other problem, however. As Gadgets observed, if they were really smart, they'd sell it to both sides—

the Russians wouldn't care who else got it as long as they did.

Brognola had a solution for that, too.

"We'd like one or two of them, the leader preferably, alive."

"Alive!" Lyons's voice was incredulous.

"Alive," Brognola repeated firmly. "He doesn't have to be in perfect condition. Just well enough to be conscious for a few hours of questioning."

"How can you be sure he'll tell us anything?"

"He'll tell, Carl. He'll tell."

15

The state of California used to be mainly desert. The desert had included virtually all of what is now known as Southern California. It had also included most of the central region of the state and had extended into parts of Northern California.

Of course, that was before such things as canals and aqueducts and deep wells had been installed, engineering feats that had changed the natural climate and topography of the state.

G.M. knew all about deserts.

He had lived for three years in one of the worst. Three summers and three winters in what was a real heavyweight as deserts went, one that hadn't been changed in two hundred years of digging wells and building canals.

Death Valley.

Located in the lower portion of the middle third of California, Death Valley stretched clear to the Nevada state line.

No canals or aqueducts ran there, and wells were productive in only a couple of places. Some of the water that was found was poisonous, brackish stuff that sickened or killed any animal that drank it.

In the summertime a relentless sun burned the landscape. A little settlement in Death Valley called Furnace Creek frequently had the hottest temperatures in the nation. Sand dunes, twisted creosote bushes and granite boulders absorbed the desert sun until they too became vessels for the heat.

In the winter it was cold and desolate.

Yet, to many, the desolation had a stark beauty. The desert austerity became a purity of sorts. Its emptiness caused the same boundless effect, the same feeling of the insignificance of a single human life, as one felt in the middle of an ocean, or gazing into the infinity of a starlit night.

The desert had been there before mankind. It would be there afterward as well.

By and large the people who lived in Death Valley were a hardy bunch. They were self-sufficient and had a perverse pride in the harshness of the climate. A good many of them drove four-wheel-drive vehicles. Most of the rest drove pickup trucks. Nobody went anywhere without water, often carrying it in so-called ten-gallon ''jeep cans'' or ''jerry cans'' secured to their vehicles by metal straps.

Nobody who knew the desert, that is, because to know her was to respect her.

But not everybody knew, or respected.

Every season somebody would make that last and fatal mistake. Usually it was some damn-fool tourist who'd have a breakdown on one of the desert roads. And the tourist wouldn't have water. And then, instead of finding the nearest shade—which would usually be next to the car—and waiting for either help or nightfall, the poor fool would try to walk out.

In the old days the result would be one more tangle of bones bleaching in the indifferent sun. Now, though, only the souls would be left; the bodies were recovered.

Usually.

G.M. had lived in Death Valley. He had lived in an abandoned mine in the Panamint Mountains after his release from prison the last time. Though he didn't know it, the location wasn't far from the Barker Ranch, where the Charles Manson "family" had been captured.

While he had never learned to appreciate Death Valley's beauty, G.M. did learn its hardships and how to survive them.

The desert didn't favor the good, or punish the bad. Cruelly impartial, it treated them all the same. But its solitude did have one effect on anyone who wasn't comfortable with being alone with his conscience.

It drove such a person slowly and inexorably mad.

When he had left Death Valley, G.M. was completely, certifiably insane. He had gone to live with his brother, Pig, down in the San Diego area.

Pig, who looked like a stouter, tattooed version of G.M., was a meth dealer in 'Dago. He had even gone on a couple of raids with G.M., just for kicks when there wasn't anything else to do.

Maybe he'd ask Pig if he wanted to come along and witness the big score. And it would be a big one, the biggest ever. Eight million big ones. Eight million plus the woman. G.M. grinned.

The deal was going to go down in Death Valley. That's what he would tell the government man, and that's what he would tell the Russians.

Now, thought G.M., I need a plan.

"I need a plan," he said aloud.

A few feet away, Slimy gave a start. His eyes met Whip's. The latter shrugged.

G.M. ignored them. Saying his thoughts out loud was a habit he had developed when he had lived in the desert. When nobody was around, it didn't matter if a person spoke aloud or just thought.

Sometimes, when he was just thinking, it turned out he had been talking. Other times he would believe he had spoken when, in fact, it had all been in his head.

No matter. Soon he was going to have eight million bucks, four from the Americans and four from the Russians.

And Sara.

But he still needed a plan.

One thing was sure. They would try to double-cross him. He knew that. That was how they thought. The government man had given in too easily, and that meant he would be sending a team to kill G.M. and take back the papers. The Russians might try to do the same thing. That was why he needed a plan.

Then it came to him.

"The Russians," he said aloud. "The Commies."

This time neither Slimy nor Whip looked up.

Yes, thought G.M. excitedly, that was it. He would play them off against one another. He'd tell the Americans to show up with the four million and Sara. And he'd tell the Commies to show up with their four million.

The Commies and the Americans would kill one another.

"They'll all be dead. And I'll have the eight million and the girl," he said aloud.

Or did he just think it, he wondered.

16

David Ivanchenko gave a grim nod of satisfaction.

The passport he carried gave his name as David I. Van-Sheck, as did the California driver's license, the Auto Club card and several assorted credit cards. The photos on the passport and the driver's license were perfect, although he'd aged somewhat. Any cop who stopped him and examined the ID would be satisfied.

He had chosen the alias himself, and he was pleased with it. To his way of thinking, the name was both humorous and disdainful.

The humor was based on the fact that the alias was so similar to his true name. The disdain came from how easy it was to fool the officials in this nation of bloated consumers, a race that placed individual liberty and happiness above the good of the state.

When he had announced his chosen cover name, his adjunct at the KGB had expressed concern.

"Surely, Comrade Ivanchenko, it is an unnecessary risk to take on a name so similar to your own."

Ivanchenko dismissed this with a wave of his hand. He fancied himself a sort of Soviet James Bond. In the past five years he had even achieved some success in cultivating the image within the narrow professional circle of the KGB.

He lit a cigarette and replied. "In the Soviet Union it might be that to do so would be a risk. But in the West...no, comrade, I gamble nothing by that. Besides," he paused, affecting what he thought was a dashing lack of concern, "it has a certain...style about it. A flair. Wouldn't you agree?"

"Your reputation for reckless bravery is without question, comrade. But is it not likely that the Americans will investigate a name that sounds so similar? In our country the state computers would seize on such a...a soundalike in an instant."

"America is not like that."

"How can you be sure, Comrade Ivanchenko?"

"I have studied the Americans, comrade. I know how they think and how they act."

"And how is that, comrade?"

"They are an nation of sentimentalists, weak and sotted."

"Sentimentalists—even weak and sotted sentimentalists—can design computer programs to detect soundalikes."

Ivanchenko smiled. "My friend, it is likely an American lawyer could successfully argue that no spy would ever choose a name so similar to his own Russian name, and therefore it is proof I am *not* an agent. And a jury would probably believe it and acquit me."

His colleague allowed a grin. "Well, comrade, if you say so. I, too, have heard stories of the American legal system."

Ivanchenko turned serious for a moment. "Never forget, comrade, that American attorneys and their so-called free press are our best allies in the struggle against Western imperialism. Both are used with great success to divide the nation, turning the people against themselves."

Apart from his carefully cultivated image as a dashing secret agent, the hard fact of the matter was that David

Ivanchenko, aka David I. VanSheck, was indeed as competent and ruthless an agent as the USSR could produce.

Physically he stood six feet exactly, with granite features. His body was hard and muscular; his strength nothing less than prodigious.

Mentally he was even more ruthless than he was arrogant. Moreover, he was willing to do whatever it took to achieve his goals. It made him an ideal candidate for the specialty he practiced within the KGB.

Wet work, it was called. The ''wet'' stood for the peculiar slippery wetness of blood and viscera, a fitting symbol of killing and torturing. The man who called himself David I. VanSheck was one of the KGB's top wet agents.

Ivanchenko had been an athlete in the Soviet sports machine when the KGB had first recruited him.

Originally he had wanted to be a boxer. He had planned to win the gold at the World Games and then at the Olympics for the glory of Moscow. Later, however, he had realized that the rewards for Soviet boxers, unlike other sports, were few beyond brain damage. And given his phenomenal athletic ability—not to mention his ego—he had made a change.

Decathlon.

The most versatile of all sports, the decathlon was one area where the Soviet Union's domination wasn't complete yet. Ivanchenko had set his sights on the gold and had trained with a ruthless determination that was nothing less than fanatical. He had become a man obsessed.

A quirk of fate had led to his recruitment by the KGB.

Another athlete, excellent in his own right but inferior to Ivanchenko, was chosen for the World Games. The man who would soon become a KGB agent was relegated to the position of an alternate.

He had appealed the decision of the sports administrators, despite the risk of permanent alienation that invoking such a process involved.

The appeal had been denied. Ivanchenko was superior in most of the events of the decathlon, to be sure. However, the other man's experience had given him an intangible edge, judges had said. Politics, the young athlete had realized, weren't unheard of in the Soviet sports apparatus. The ambitious ex-boxer's hopes of glory had apparently been crushed.

A brutal injury had resurrected those hopes.

In the closing weeks of training, while practicing for the pole vault, the other man's fiberglass pole had shattered as it had flexed to whip him up and over the horizontal bar. The lower portion of the pole had impaled the falling athlete through the abdomen. He had lived, but barely.

The alternate, David Ivanchenko, had stepped in for the competition. The mystery of how a new and carefully guarded pole could fail in such a manner was never solved.

The KGB had known, however. One of the top-placed executives, a man named Rigert, recognized talent when he saw it. This was talent of a different sort, however, the talent to do anything necessary to win.

Rigert had had Ivanchenko brought to him. He had made the young athlete an offer. Go to work for Rigert, in the most secret branch of the most secret organization in the world, or go to the gulag for the violent assault on the other athlete.

At first Ivanchenko had been confident that such a charge couldn't be proven. Later, as he had learned about Rigert's power, he had realized that it could, indeed, be proven, and that if they were in need of evidence, it would be found. Or made.

Ivanchenko had accepted Rigert's "offer."

He had become a member of Rigert's ultrasecret group. There his phenomenal talents were concentrated on the arts of wet work. He had quickly become Rigert's main undercover enforcer in the U.S., the man who kept Russian agents in line and neutralized any threats to their spy apparatus.

Now Ivanchenko reviewed the facts of his present mission.

A Soviet spy somewhere in the vast network within the United States had landed a big fish. Or, if not yet landed, had at least hooked it. The catch consisted of documents relating to a key part of the American defense program. They were the genuine article; Soviet scientists had been given a sample and were champing at the bit to get the rest. The price was steep, incredible, in fact, but the papers were of such vital significance that Moscow had approved the expenditure.

Ivanchenko's orders, as formulated by the Executive Committee of the KGB, would be transmitted personally by courier. That meant it was a top-priority mission.

To use an international courier required that a messenger be dispatched from KGB headquarters itself. The orders could only be transmitted by face-to-face conversation. The process served several purposes. It minimized the chance of interception, and it assured those in the Committee that the instructions were indeed given and received. Perhaps most of all, however, it gave particular emphasis to the importance of the mission.

As required, Ivanchenko and the courier arranged to meet so that the instructions could be delivered personally.

The meeting occurred near the ocean on a beach. Both men wore swimsuits; each carried a radio tuned to a different station. They faced out to sea as they talked.

"It is to be stressed that this mission is of utmost importance, comrade," the courier began.

Aren't they all, thought Ivanchenko. Aloud, he said gravely, "I understand."

"Your mission is to ensure the transfer of the documents from the American mercenary robbers to agents of the Soviet Union."

The wet agent was puzzled. "We are simply to shepherd the exchange, then? To act as bodyguards?"

"No, comrade. There is another dimension as well. We have information that the American government has dispatched a team of killers to block the transmission of these vital materials."

"I see."

"You are first to see that the exchange of the documents for the money can occur. Then you are to capture and interrogate both the mercenary robbers and, if it is possible, one or more members of the American kill squad."

"Do the instructions suggest how that is to be accomplished?"

"Yes, comrade, to a certain extent. It is stressed that the result is of greater importance than the methods. Nonetheless, the Committee has seen fit to make certain suggestions."

I bet they have, thought Ivanchenko sarcastically. They don't care how it gets done as long as it gets done. And then they give me their "suggestions." If I employ another approach, which will most certainly be a better way, and I fail, the gulag is the best I could hope for. If I follow their suggestions, the chance of failure is increased, but they must be more lenient.

Ivanchenko shook his head in disgust, but didn't comment. The courier looked at him curiously, then continued.

"It is suggested you take a squad of six men, all wet trained."

"I choose them," Ivanchenko demanded.

The courier shrugged. "You choose. Use only American or European firearms, ones that are commonly known and available throughout the world. It is important that the Americans not be able to establish any kind of link to the Soviet Union."

"Go on."

"The Committee has learned that the men who have the documents will attempt to arrange a meeting with American agents. The purpose will be to offer the plans back to the United States in lieu of selling them to us.

"This meeting will occur after the exchange with our agents. The Committee specifies that you are to first allow our agents to obtain the documents. The documents *must* be obtained."

"And then?"

"And then capture these American mercenaries, the ones who are selling the plans."

"Capture? Or kill?"

"First capture. The Committee is eager to learn everything the mercenaries know about the documents. You are to conduct an interrogation without limits to determine that."

"Without limits?" Ivanchenko repeated. "They will not survive, of course."

"Of course," said the courier calmly. "They should not survive. The Committee simply wants to know as much about these plans and where they were obtained as is possible. It is anticipated you will liquidate any who survive the interrogation. Both the money and the plans can then be given to a courier for delivery to the Committee."

"What about the American kill squad?"

"Your interrogation of the others will confirm exactly when and where the meeting with the American squad will occur."

Ivanchenko smiled. "And then we will attend the meeting," he said carelessly.

"Precisely, comrade. If, as anticipated, they arrive after the exchange with our agents, you are to do the same thing to them."

"Interrogate them? Or just kill them?"

"Interrogate them. It is a rare opportunity to, shall we say, 'debrief' highly placed United States assassins." The courier gave a thin, mirthless smile. "It is comparable in some ways to the U.S. coming into possession of one of our MiG fighter planes during the Vietnam conflict."

Ivanchenko saw the similarities in each case. He nodded thoughtfully. "Much was learned by the U.S. from that MiG," he mused.

The courier nodded. "Much could be learned here."

"About what? What is to be the focus of the questioning?" inquired Ivanchenko.

"The subject of the interrogation will not concern the documents of course. But the Committee sees this as a chance to learn a great deal about the enforcement component of the American intelligence apparatus."

"Why not just read the *Washington Post*?" Ivanchenko asked, back in his role as a dashing and disdainful agent. "The American press seems to know more about their intelligence community than anyone else does."

The courier allowed a smile but didn't comment. "Of course," he continued, "the documents are the first priority. Should the American killers arrive during the exchange, you are to protect the exchange and secure the documents by whatever means necessary."

Ivanchenko thought it over.

The plan seemed simple, the mission straightforward. Bodyguard the exchange, then torture and kill the men who had the plans. Do the same when the American kill squad arrived.

A question occurred to him. "Do the Americans—the American kill squad—expect Soviet intervention?"

The courier shook his head. "Our information is that they do not. They believe the mercenaries have decided to sell the plans back to their own government. We believe they have no knowledge that the KGB is interested."

Later, looking back on the conversation, Ivanchenko was pleased with the courier's carefully chosen words. So the Americans weren't aware that the KGB would be there. That meant it would be an easy mission. There would be the chance for combat and killing, but the odds would be entirely on his side. The thrill of a battle that he undoubtedly would win was the best of both worlds.

He considered the prospects. The end result would be another cash bonus for him—Russia's avowed socialist government employed some very capitalist devices to reward success—and perhaps another medal to his credit back in the Soviet Union.

And the risk was minimal.

It was a good life, Ivanchenko thought contentedly.

17

"Goddamn lamebrains, you'd think they'd at least give us the right hotel," one of the delivery men from the Rolan Refrigeration Company grumbled.

"What seems to be the problem?" inquired the manager of the Bonaventure.

"There's nothing wrong with the ice machine on that floor," the head workman said. "It's working fine. Any better and you'd be building igloos up there."

"I told you there was no work order," the manager said pointedly.

"Lamebrains," muttered the workman again as he and his partner trundled the new ice machine onto the flat tailgate of their truck. Then, with the whine of equipment, he raised the tailgate to the level of the truck bed, and the two grumbling workmen pushed it back inside the cargo area.

IN LYONS'S ROOM, Gadgets was rinsing out the bathtub where the dead Russian had so recently been stashed.

"You know," he observed over his shoulder to Politician, "the Chief doesn't miss a trick. Those agents made real good delivery *and* pickup men. It was very neatly done."

"How so, amigo?"

"Well, ice machines hold ice. Ice sometimes becomes water, and—"

"I thought ice was always water," cut in Lyons from outside the bathroom. The Ironman was always quick to correct Able Team's resident genius, even if it was only on a minor point of semantics. "It's just frozen water as opposed to liquid water, right?"

Gadgets rolled his eyes and gave a long-suffering sigh. "As I was saying," he continued, "when the ice melts it becomes water in its liquid state. Water tends to leak out of things, and so the ice machine is designed to be watertight," he said in his most professorial voice. "And—"

"If it's watertight, it's bloodtight as well," Lyons finished for him.

"And the same design would contain other fluids as well," Gadgets went on calmly, as though no interruption had occurred. "Not to mention the fact that an ice machine like that is big enough to hold a body quite nicely."

"Is a frog's ass watertight?" mused Blancanales.

"Huh?" said Lyons.

"They used to say that in boot camp," replied Politician with a wink. "They told us they wanted us to be 'tight.' You know, to stick together, to help out your buddy. 'As tight as a frog's ass,' they'd say. And how tight was that? Why, watertight, of course."

"Do tell." Lyons gave a shrug as he thumbed a puttylike spackling paste into the last of the 9 mm craters in the wall. "I missed out on that little gem of information."

The three Able Team warriors were waiting for the final details of the exchange with the marauders. Lyons answered when Brognola's call came through.

"Able here."

Brognola's voice was all crisp, all business. "The marauders have made contact. The exchange of the plans for the money will occur in Death Valley at 1900 hours. That's about five and a half hours from now.

"Go to the roof of the hotel at exactly 1345 hours. An LAPD chopper will meet you there. It will airlift you to an army transport helicopter that should be on standby, ready and waiting. The pilot has been briefed. He's trustworthy. He'll get you to the rendezvous point up in the high desert."

Lyons nodded, forgetting that Brognola couldn't see him. "Ten-four, Chief. Anything else?"

"Yes. The army chopper will have your supplies and equipment already on board, including topographic maps of the area. Your job is to get in fast and overpower the marauders with minimal casualties to them and hopefully none to you."

"You still want them alive, then, I take it?"

Lyons's voice was grim; going up against this kind of foe was bad enough under the circumstances, but doing so under conditions of "try not to hurt them" made things more difficult.

"That's affirmative."

"May I ask why?"

"You may. And I can even give you a partial answer. One reason is that we want to find out exactly what contact they've had with the Russians, as well as any other planned dissemination of the materials."

"And?" prompted the Ironman.

"And we have to consider the possibility that they might not even have the documents with them when you make the rendezvous. It's possible that they may suspect a trap, and, as a precaution, left the papers in a safe place."

"Or they may have duplicates somewhere else," suggested Lyons, reiterating the theory that Gadgets had advanced earlier.

"Yes. We considered that. It's quite likely that another set of the documents is in the hands of a third party, an accomplice who has instructions to send them somewhere if he doesn't receive other orders by a certain time."

"So you want them alive."

"Alive, or reasonably so. As I said earlier, that doesn't necessarily mean completely undamaged. I couldn't send you into a situation like this with orders not to defend yourselves."

"Gee, thanks."

Brognola continued, unruffled. "Still, if possible, we'd like a couple of them still breathing so we can persuade them to unburden their consciences of these and similar matters."

"Persuade?"

"A second chopper with a team of specialists will be standing by at a discreet but readily accessible location. They can be on the scene as soon as you've secured it and things are under control. You'll deliver the survivors to them, to these specialists, and be extracted yourselves."

"Specialists," Lyons repeated, more to himself than to his commander.

He knew what the term meant, and he didn't like it.

Interrogators.

The Ironman had been on the receiving end of a couple of interrogations himself. It was a significant understatement to say that he hadn't enjoyed it. Moreover, he didn't enjoy being a principal in the same process now. And, to his way of thinking, that was what he would be by aiding and abetting in the delivery of the marauders to the "specialists."

Still, he knew that such tactics were a necessary evil. The threat of nuclear war was a reality. One didn't make it go away by ignoring it, or by loving the Russians, or by soliciting meaningless assurances from the Soviets that they weren't going to build more than a certain number of hydrogen bombs.

Sure thing, pal.

Promises and love were all well and good, of course, provided one had the necessary hardware to make any alternative approach too costly for the other side.

The documents were part of that hardware. A stroke of fate had placed them in the hands of these marauders, and fate, in the form of Lyons, Blancanales and Schwarz, was about to snatch them back again. The interrogation bit was nothing more than one part of that process, set in motion by the scumbags themselves.

They'd made the first move, Lyons thought. They'd opened the door. They can hardly be surprised if we walk through it as far as we have to. And if that includes using "specialists" such as the "I-squad," that's the way it has to be, he thought.

Still, that didn't mean he had to like it. Aloud, he said, "Question, Chief."

"Shoot."

"Do you expect any intervention by the Russians in the rendezvous?"

"Negative."

"Why not?"

"We now know, of course, that the marauders have made contact with a Soviet agent."

"Didn't you already know that?" Lyons queried.

"Initially, when the negotiations were going on, we were told by the leader—he calls himself G.M.—that he had made contact with a Russian agent. At that time, however, we were inclined to regard it as a bluff, a tactic to scare us into upping the ante, so to speak."

"But?"

"As I said before, other sources known to our intelligence community provided indications that such a contact may actually have occurred."

"What about the guy in our room? That's a pretty good indication, I'd say," observed Lyons dryly.

"That confirmed it of course," agreed Brognola brusquely. "Moreover, it confirmed the presence of a leak somewhere in either the Justice Department or the Department of Defense."

"How so?"

"Simple. How did the Russians know you were going to be involved unless there was a leak? Anyway, their information was apparently only hours behind our own decision to deploy you. That's how the, uh, one-man welcoming committee happened to be in your room."

Lyons glanced at his two partners. "Is it too much to ask whether this leak you referred to has been found and plugged? Do you know who it is at least?"

Brognola's voice sounded cold and thin. "My counterpart in the Justice Department tells me the leak was, in fact, found."

"Has it been plugged?"

"Negative. Not yet anyway."

"Why not?" demanded Lyons angrily.

"Use your head, Ironman," snapped Brognola. "It will be plugged after it is used to transmit erroneous information back to the Soviet Union. Information that sounds vitally important, and close enough to the truth to be credible, but is misleading in several significant aspects. In other words, we'll use their own tool against them."

"Makes sense," Lyons reluctantly acknowledged.

Brognola continued. "None of that is relevant here, however. What is relevant is that you get up there, get the documents if possible and get the bodies—alive—in any event."

Lyons's voice was somber. "What about Janie?"

"Good thing you asked. I almost forgot." Brognola took a deep breath.

"So tell me."

"He wants Sara, so we'll give him Sara. At least enough to get back the documents or capture the assholes."

"Are you serious?"

"Your Janie—his Sara—will be on the chopper, Ironman."

A cold, hard knot began to form in the pit of Lyons's stomach. He started to object, then checked himself.

Brognola, was, after all, their commander. On that principle alone such an objection, when they were running so close to the wire, would amount to insubordination.

More than that, however, the Chief was a master strategist. And, though it was part of the game that Brognola might sacrifice them—or at least throw them into a situation where survival was unlikely if not impossible—he would not do the same with an innocent civilian.

If he called it that way, there had to be a reason.

"What's . . . Sara going to be doing, Chief?" The words came out in a soft, husky, almost distracted tone.

Brognola's reply was smooth. "She'll be on hand to make the exchange, Carl."

"Say again?"

"You'll be riding with four million dollars, all packed in army duffel bags. However many duffel bags it takes to hold four million. Sara will be on hand to make the exchange."

"Is this for real?"

"Look, I know how this must affect you, Carl. I understand your concern. And I'm working on a way to keep Janie out of it as much as possible."

Lyons didn't reply.

"However, so you know, I've agreed that . . . Sara will make the exchange."

"She'll be in the thick of it."

"Maybe. Maybe not. Part of that will depend on how things break from your end."

"Yeah."

"Good luck, Ironman."

"Yeah. Able out."

18

Once, when he was a kid of about eight, Carl Lyons had stayed with his grandparents for a week. Every morning Grandma had given him what she called "porridge."

The kind old lady had never heated the stuff up enough. It was always a cold, congealed, chunk of gluey glop in his bowl. Even now, years later, he could remember the feeling of that fist-sized lump sitting in his tummy.

It took hours to digest.

The young Lyons used to imagine the stuff forming into the walls of an ancient city in the pit of his stomach. Then, for the next two hours, he visualized his stomach acids, dressed like Roman warriors, laying siege to the walls of glop.

His imaginary legions suffered unbelievable casualties in the assault. A hail of arrows would come from the defenders of the blob. Ladders flung up against the walls by his troops were hurled backward. The scene would soon be littered with the dead and dying and punctuated with the screams of the wounded.

Finally a single Roman warrior would make it to the top of the wall.

Not surprisingly, that soldier looked like Carl Lyons. His imaginary body resembled a blond Steve Reeves or Reg Park, movie stars who had played in the Hercules films of the fifties, the Arnold Schwarzeneggers or Bill Pearls of his day.

Moments later that soldier would be joined by another.

This one was almost as well built and looked a lot like Jimmy Kowalski, who coincidentally happened to be the young Ironman's best friend at that time. Together, using the Roman short sword and shield, the two young legionnaires would chop and thrust and parry in pitched battle. Relentlessly they would drive a wedge into the Goths and Vandals of the porridge.

Muscular arms and massive shoulders flexed in the mortal combat.

Iron clanged above the screams of the gladiators.

Slowly, painfully, the tide would begin to turn. The other legionnaires would take heart from the invincible courage of the two who had breached the wall. Finally the glop defenders would be forced to give ground to the "Carl" and "Jimmy" of the Roman legions. When that happened, the rest of the legionnaires could swarm over the fortress, and the glop would be theirs.

Carl and Jimmy always got wounded but never died. And, although their wounds bled copiously, they always seemed to heal quickly.

"It's a long way from my heart," they would say as they shrugged, using a phrase that would find its way into Lyons's adult vocabulary as well, though usually in a self-deprecating context.

When it was finally over, after two or three hours of vicious combat, the sticky glop would be vanquished, crushed, beneath their victorious Roman heels. Then, and only then, would Carl's tummy fully recover from breakfast.

Maybe it didn't really take two or three hours, but it sure seemed like it.

Nonetheless, the cost of victory was prodigious. While the battle raged, the young Carl Lyons lived with the clammy lump in his gut, a queasy, immobilizing presence that sapped his will.

As he walked across the cracked cement of the helipad to where the U.S. Army chopper waited, Lyons felt that old feeling. It was as if all those bowls of porridge had been pressed into one clammy, dense blob, a blob that now reposed in the pit of his stomach.

He dreaded the prospect of seeing Janie, especially under the circumstances of this meeting.

It was that fear—the grim anticipation—that gave him the porridgelike feeling in his gut. Only it was ten times worse than any he had felt as a kid. Like a black hole on the far edge of the universe, a pocket of ultradense matter that even sucked light rays into itself by sheer gravitational force, this lump drained his energy and even left him feeling cold.

Somebody had once observed that ex-wives really weren't like sharks or grizzly bears; after all, they couldn't eat you.

Whoever said that didn't know Janie, Lyons thought.

No, he amended hastily, that wasn't completely fair. It wasn't Janie's fault any more than it was his. It wasn't anybody's fault. Two well-meaning people had tried to put two pieces together and had thought the pieces would stay together forever. Only the pieces hadn't stayed together.

Lyons knew that most of what he felt was conditioned, a behavior pattern that he had allowed to form. A bad habit, in other words. And he knew that the way to get over those bad habits was to practice good ones until they replaced the bad ones.

Be cool, Ironman, he told himself. There's nothing to be afraid of. This is just a mission like any other mission—you just happen to know one of the bystanders.

Still, it was comforting to recall that in the final analysis ex-wives couldn't eat you.

The chopper loomed before him. Shit, he thought, it's a big bastard. Lyons hadn't been in the military, and he didn't know anything about these toys of war, even though he'd ridden in his share of them during his exploits with Stony Man Farm.

He'd heard Blancanales use the term "CH-43-C" in a context that he deduced might refer to this helicopter, or one similar. Gadgets had nodded and said something about "Chocaw" or "Sikorsky."

Whatever the label, this one was a bulbous, ungainly bastard. It reminded him of a misshapen olive-drab banana with rotors like dragonfly wings on its top at each end. Lyons quickened his pace, striding with a grim determination to hit the blow head-on, like a running back getting ready to be hit hard but determined to stay on his feet.

He was aware that Gadgets and Blancanales had dropped back, first slowing, then stopping, as if to give him a moment's privacy despite the ticking downward of the mission clock.

The cargo door to the chopper was open, and through it, well above him due to the size of the beast, Lyons could see a human figure. As he got closer, he saw it was a woman.

Janie.

She stood facing away from him, with her arms folded across her stomach. It was as if she was protecting herself from a cold wind, although the afternoon was warm. Her shoulders appeared tense, and she was looking resolutely away from him.

Can I do this? Lyons wondered. The lump in his gut felt colder and heavier than ever.

As he got closer, he saw that she was wearing tailored shorts of a khaki material. His immediate impulse was critical—what the hell was she doing wearing that kind of garb to a firefight. Then he checked himself. Brognola had undoubtedly specified the clothing. Probably he had based the choice on something the shrinks had deduced about the psychotic features held by this lowlife, G.M.

Accurate or not, it was better to go with the odds than against them.

Her blond hair was lighter than he remembered. Her legs looked strong and fit. She must be playing a lot of tennis, he thought.

She didn't turn to face him. He clambered into the chopper.

"Jane?" His voice came out in a croak. "Janie?"

Still she didn't move. He cleared his throat and tried it again.

"Jane, it's me. Carl."

He saw the tension go out of her shoulders. Then, with what looked like the deliberate motion of sheer determination, she turned to face him.

Lyons stared. His mind refused to accept the data his eyes transmitted.

She was attractive, all right, as he had remembered. She was the right height, she had blond hair and blue eyes, and she looked as if she could have a hell of a smile.

But she wasn't Jane Odom.

19

Stunned, Carl Lyons stared at the woman.

She regarded him with a mixture of curiosity, apprehension and maybe just a hint of sympathy.

"Who the hell are you?" the Ironman demanded.

Her lips moved just slightly, the trace of an ironic smile.

"I'm Sara. Today, anyway."

"Where's Janie?"

"She couldn't make it. I'm her understudy." The woman smiled awkwardly and stuck out her hand. "Normally I'm Dana McKee. U.S. Marshal's Service, Special Investigations Division."

Dumbfounded, Lyons took her hand and shook it. "Who...?" he began, then realized he'd already asked that question. "How... what are you doing here?"

"I gather I'm playing the role of your ex-wife, being bait for some psycho robber spy. Otherwise," she gave a rueful grin, "same old shit, as they say."

Neither of them spoke for several moments.

Lyons turned his head to one side and stared out the cargo opening of the chopper. The lump in his gut was gone, but his system was charged with adrenaline. The effect was like having butterflies in his stomach, assuming that the butterflies were all angry, meth-charged speed freaks.

He felt two kinds of relief. One was that Janie wasn't here, which meant he wouldn't have to face her. Another was relief that she was safe.

He also felt, he admitted, just a twinge of regret. In addition, he was angered by the abrupt turn of events. Pissed off, to put it bluntly. And his initial reaction was to meet the stress of this turn of events by headlong anger.

To attack, in other words.

Whoa, Ironman, he thought suddenly. Stay loose. Move with it, not against it. That way you can turn it back at them if need be, like t'ai chi. Also it will buy you time to sort things out in your mind.

He looked at the woman and forced a grin. "So," he said at last, "do you come here often?"

"All the time," she responded lightly.

"Then would you be so good as to kindly tell me just what the hell is going on?"

"Sure. Somebody in the Justice Department needed a blonde, five-seven, mid-thirties. Actually, the blond part was optional. Hairdressers were on standby. The person had to have some law-enforcement or military background, and security clearances were a must."

Lyons stared at her.

"So," Dana continued, "they fed the input into the computers and came up with a few possibilities. I guess I'm the winner. Or loser, depending on how it goes."

"And your job is?"

"To impersonate another woman—who I understand used to be...related to you in the legal sense—who was going to be used as bait for some psycho who has stolen plans to the ultimate atomic bomb, or something. The guy who briefed me got real hazy on that part of it."

"What did he look like?"

"Who?"

"The guy who briefed you."

Dana described him. "Said his name was Brognola," she concluded.

Lyons frowned, trying to piece the times together. "When did all this happen?"

"Yesterday. That is, I was briefed yesterday. I was given a haircut—to match Jane's—and then put on a flight out here. I was kept on standby until the final decision was made to put me in."

"When was that?" Lyons demanded, wondering if Brognola had known all along that Janie wasn't going to be there. Even as the thought occurred to him, however, he discounted it. That kind of switch wasn't Brognola's style. Some things you don't joke with, especially where a mission was involved.

"What?"

"When was that? When did you get the go-ahead?"

"Right now. Maybe five minutes ago, that is. It was one of those 'hurry up and wait' deals. You know? The 'you probably won't be going but we need everything ready in case you do' routine. Then I got the nod, and five minutes later you're here."

Lyons tried to digest the information. It proved as indigestible as his Grandma's porridge, in the short run, anyway.

Out of the corner of his eye he saw Blancanales and Gadgets approaching the helicopter.

Fuck it.

It was just too much to assimilate. Brognola must have had his reasons for playing it this way. Maybe it had to do with last-minute conversations with G.M., or with Janie. Or, hell, maybe with the President. Whatever it was, the Chief would have some reason other than to pull a mind fuck on Lyons.

It could wait, he thought. Let's just get down to business. None of this will mean shit when the firefight starts. That was what counted now. Time to worry about the rest later, assuming he survived. And if he didn't, it wouldn't matter, would it?

He suddenly realized that was what was bothering him.

They *did* have a firefight ahead of them. And, unlike the television and movie heroes, they were very vulnerable. You hold a .223 round in your hand, he thought, and then think of that little thing screaming at you at several thousand feet per second. Suddenly your own skin seems very fragile indeed.

All courage meant was being able to handle the fear, or more accurately, to handle the realization that you could be killed or maimed at any moment, and that it would hurt like hell when it happened. Different people did it in different ways. Put it out of your mind, joke about it, work yourself up into a berserker's frenzy, pray—they were all just techniques to avoid being immobilized by fear.

Today they would confront an enemy.

Today some people would probably die. It could be them, or it could be the enemy.

Lyons had no faith in Brognola's prediction that the Russians wouldn't be there. Something in his own mind, a warrior's sixth sense perhaps, told him otherwise. So as far as he was concerned, he was headed for a firefight.

He realized that what had been bothering him was the distraction of Janie's presence in the whole thing. Coming hard on the heels of his visit to Margaret's grave, it had taken his mind off the real matter at hand.

Well, he was back to the matter at hand now, and that meant getting ready for battle.

Finally he looked back at the woman who looked so much like Jane in some ways and so utterly different in others.

"One last thing," he said. His voice was cold, all pro.

"What is it?"

"Are you trained? Can you shoot?"

"If you mean what I think you mean, yes. I've been through special weapons training. I'm a black belt in tae kwon do, and I've had eight years with the U.S. Marshal's Service. And—" she gave a slight smile "—I had three years of waitressing at Denny's."

"And before that?"

"None of your business." Her voice had become cool, her gaze one of frank appraisal. "So you're the one they call the Ironman," she said after a pause. Her voice didn't contain any inflection he could identify.

"I'm the one."

"Well, how about you, Carl? Can *you* shoot?"

Lyons regarded her grimly. "Well enough."

It wasn't exactly an original line; Lyons remembered a certain female FBI agent who had used the same cool response to a similar question he had asked. However, he didn't feel like elaborating. And if Dana didn't like it, she could shove it.

She apparently realized when to press an advantage, and when to back off. "Well, we'll soon see, won't we?" she commented lightly.

"That we will." Lyons gave a curt nod at his two partners and made his way to a seat.

Minutes later they were airborne.

20

They talked, and then they waited.

During the five-odd hours that had elapsed since lift-off in L.A., the chopper had taken them to a desolate spot in the upper Mojave Desert. That was to be the "staging area," where they would make the last minute preparations and stand by while first the hours and then the minutes and then the seconds ticked down to the final approach.

Actually the hop from L.A. had been short, just over an hour. The rest of the time had been taken up by the briefing and the waiting.

The former had been more of a brainstorming session than a traditional briefing.

In a mission where so little was known, and where the orders were to capture rather than kill, it was impossible to map out a battle plan. Instead, they spent the time trying to anticipate all the possible variations that could greet them, and to start thinking about how to handle each one.

Or, as Lyons put it, "Just try to figure out all the ways it could turn to shit on us."

Mainly the planning filled the time while they waited.

Every fighting man Lyons had ever met—every one in the world probably, he figured—had experienced the same thing. Every soldier, every cop, every secret agent, every astronaut, hell, every one of the doers as opposed to the watchers, knew the feeling. And it could all be summed up in a single sentence: you never knew if it was going to be a go until it went.

Lyons and the others knew that most missions were little parts in big machines. A lot of factors affected the "go/no go" decision, most of which were not known to the poor bastards who would be doing the going. So they learned to wait in a curious kind of limbo, knowing that if it went it would be hell, but if it didn't it would be nothing. It was enough to drive any sane man crazy.

The scrub signal could come at any time. But if it didn't, they were all "go."

It didn't come by 1600 hours. A million things rioted in Lyons's mind, though outwardly he appeared calm. Bravery was a habit, he knew, and part of that habit was looking as if he were brave. "Act as if you have faith, and faith will be given to you," he could remember his mother saying.

Maybe Mom wasn't too far off that one, he thought.

He looked over at Blancanales. The former Black Beret was lying in the shade of the chopper. His arms were folded across his chest, his eyes closed. Next to him lay an M-16 and a light pack. Guy looks like he's dozing, Lyons thought. Hell, he looks almost, well, serene.

1630 hours. No call-off. Empty your brain. Turn off the TV set in your mind. Forget Janie and Margaret and all the others dead and living. This is now and now is your life.

Would they be alive two hours from now?

Probably.

1700 hours. The sun began to cast long shadows over the vast fabric of the desert. Lyons looked at the empty beauty. It made him feel small, and a little lonely. But there was no fear.

1730 hours. Nothing. Empty your mind. This is nothing more than act and react. It's what you've been trained to do.

Nobody can guarantee results; all that matters is that you give it your best shot, that you go at it the way you've been taught.

1800 hours. Lift-off in thirty-five minutes.

Capture these guys alive?

The thought bulled its way into Lyons's mind yet again. What if they start shooting first? What if the exchange is only a sham? What if the only way is to kill or be killed?

Which was worth more, a shot at recovering the plans to the ultimate tool of national defense—and preventing the Russians from getting them—or your own life?

Lyons didn't know how he would call that one. He'd cross that bridge when he came to it. Or maybe it would be more appropriate to say *burn* that bridge when he came to it.

Don't worry about it. Whatever happens, something will happen. Besides, there could still be a call-off at any time.

1810 hours. He was ready. He wanted to go.

Finally they clambered into the chopper. Lyons noticed that Blancanales immediately found a spot on one of the metal benches. The former Black Beret sat down, feet firmly on the floor, his body upright but his back rounded and his arms folded across his stomach. Once again, as he had done outside, he shut his eyes and began to doze.

The cavernous interior was more gloomy than the outside had been. Lyons wondered why they didn't send something smaller, one of those little bastards that could swoop down and let them off.

Questions like that were a waste of time and energy, he knew. This wasn't supposed to be a "drop off and fight" activity anyway. Theoretically they were going to set down and negotiate and then, in effect, arrest.

Sure thing, Ironman.

Red lights glowed in the dark hull, providing some illumination. At the front, Lyons could make out the shapes of the pilot and another man. The copilot, thought Lyons, though whether he was actually there for that purpose wasn't clear. The scene had an eerie feeling of unreality to it—four people, one of them a woman, sitting in the red glow of a darkened chopper in the desert twilight, wondering if they would live or die.

1820 hours.

The crackle of static ran through the hull of the chopper. Lyons glanced forward. A light winked on the radio panel. In the reflected light of the instruments, Lyons could see the pilot's lips move in a response of some sort. His face was impassive as he listened. Then he said something that somehow looked like an acknowledgment and settled back to wait.

Why doesn't he tell us what that was? Lyons thought angrily. Was it a scrub? Or a delay? Then he forced himself to calm down. If it had been either of those things, the pilot would have told them.

Probably.

Blancanales still looked like he was asleep, arms still folded across his middle, head slightly forward, eyes closed. The chopper suddenly rumbled, and the noise became thunderous as the idle increased to a roar of engines and gears and rotors. Still, the former paratrooper didn't appear to notice.

"Hey, Blanc!"

It was Gadgets, shouting above the roar of the machine. The Able Team genius, himself a veteran of Vietnam, was on the other side of the chopper, parallel to Politician.

Blancanales didn't appear to hear him.

"Hey, Blanc!" Gadgets repeated, shouting louder this time.

Slowly Blancanales opened his eyes. Without moving his head more than a few degrees, he looked over at his partner in the red glow.

Gadgets, a merry grin on his face, gave the thumbs-up gesture, fist clenched, thumb extended, making a stabbing motion upward.

A slight smile spread over Blancanales's face. Slowly, almost lazily, his arms still folded across his chest, he freed the fist on the side nearest to Gadgets. Then he moved his own thumb upward and nodded in a careless, carefree acknowledgment of the gesture. Then he shut his eyes again.

Moments later the roar of the equipment got even louder, and they lifted off.

21

They came in low and fast. Or, to be more precise, as fast and low as the huge chopper could go. Lyons watched the landing spot as they made their approach. It looked eerie and deserted in the twilight.

The place was an old mining operation known as the Star Mine. It consisted of the remnants of a house and a couple of outbuildings. The house had been built from stone, using head-size chunks of the granite that littered the area. Whatever the original roof had been constructed from had long since been destroyed. The walls had fared little better; in several places they had either fallen in or been pulled down by vandals.

Still, one end of the structure remained more or less intact. A makeshift roof of two-by-sixes and corrugated iron had been built over that part of it. Beyond the stone house stood the two outbuildings. These were of more recent vintage, one built of wood and the other a steel prefabricated building. The trio of buildings was all that remained of some man's attempt at shelter from an inhospitable environment

Both newer buildings showed the effects of the desert heat and cold. Where there was wood, it had dried and splintered. On the metal one, only flakes of paint remained. Both sheds also bore bullet holes from the idle potshots of countless gun-carrying four-wheel-drive idiots who had ventured there.

Still farther away were the mine shafts. They were identifiable by the tailings of rock that had been extracted, and were now barely visible in the failing light.

They came in fast and low, but didn't attempt to conceal their approach.

The helicopter's arrival hadn't been planned as a secret; as Lyons had earlier reasoned, it wasn't a quick in-and-out raid. At least, he amended, it wasn't supposed to look like one, despite the fact that it might end up that way. As a result, they came in with lights on, according to Brognola's directions.

Just before it touched down, the chopper hesitated momentarily in midair, several feet off the ground. The engines and rotors made a deafening roar as the pilot performed some final adjustments before allowing the huge beast to settle to the rocky earth.

It all happened at once.

Lyons heard the sudden clanging of bullets striking the chopper. Then, an instant later, he realized he was hearing the sound of guns over the roar of the craft.

"Ambush!" he shouted.

"Indian country!" yelled Gadgets simultaneously, using the term popular in Vietnam to denote hostiles.

They scrabbled to a ready position in order to facilitate their bailout.

At that moment, in the glow of the instruments in the cabin, Lyons saw the pilot's head come apart in a dark-colored mess of blood and brains.

It seemed to happen in slow motion, and yet it was over in an instant. Lyons had seen headshots before, and there was never any doubt of their fatal finale—the abrupt stiffening of the body as nerves overloaded, galvanizing the muscles into rigidity; the sideways snapping of the head from the force of the impact; and the spray of dark matter as the exiting projectile ripped away skull and scalp and whatever was inside.

At the pilot's spasm, the chopper made a wild lurch to one side.

It twisted and dropped the remaining few feet to the ground, striking the rocky surface with a bone-jarring crash. The violent motion had caused the right side to impact first, and the landing gear buckled from the uneven stress.

For a few moments the ungainly beast skittered along the ridge, engines roaring. Then, as the angle increased, the forward rotor struck the ground.

The blade sheared off, but the torque of the impact whipped the machine in a violent circular motion, end around end, accompanied by the ear-splitting clamor of tortured steel against uneven granite. Finally it stopped, some twenty yards away from the original touchdown site.

The chopper came to rest on its right-hand side, heeled over at about a forty-five-degree angle. As one, the three men and Dana scrabbled for the exit at the rear of the craft.

Abruptly Gadgets stopped. "The emergency door!" he shouted, pointing in the near blackness.

Lyons was closest to it. He leaped to the downward side of the chopper and kicked the release handle. The door fell free, landing with a crash. Without hesitation, he dropped into the twilight gloom and glanced around.

All clear.

"Now!" he hissed urgently.

He moved out of the way, allowing the others to drop free. The four of them froze and peered about, letting their eyes become accustomed to the darkness.

The Ironman crouched and looked and listened.

His casual clothing was gone. The three warriors had changed into more appropriate combat garb back at the staging area—desert camou fatigues and sleeveless flak jackets. While it was true that they weren't expecting a fire-fight, the gear still seemed appropriate for their role as bodyguards and chaperons for a four-million-dollar transaction.

"What the well-dressed spy-catcher is wearing this season," as Gadgets had quipped.

Only Dana was still dressed as she had been.

That wasn't due to any feminine vanity of course. Her cover, in the role she had to play, demanded it. G.M., whoever that psycho was, seemed to have a fetish for somebody blond and fit and tanned. If that was how he liked the bait, that was how the bait had to look.

Now, however, her tanned legs looked distressingly pale in the darkness—an easy target for the snipers.

They each carried identical weapons, including Dana: M-16 rifles, with .45 ACP Government Model automatics for side arms.

The standard U.S. Army-issue M-16s were the real thing, with full-auto capability. "Autoburn," as Blancanales, the former Black Beret and Vietnam veteran always put it. Each of them had several extra clips of both the hot .223 ammunition and the "knock you down and walk all over you" .45 ACP for the handguns.

In addition, Blancanales and Gadgets had packs that contained a mysterious assortment of other pyrotechnic and explosive devices.

Lyons glanced about to make sure the others were okay. Dana's face had a dark streak; he couldn't tell whether it was blood or grime. He started to speak, then checked himself—it was a long way from her heart. As he looked, she dropped immediately into a low crouch behind a stunted brush of some sort.

Smart broad, Lyons thought.

It wasn't cover, but it was concealment.

The sagebrush wouldn't stop a bullet, of course, but it did break up the pale outline of her legs. In the same glance he realized that she had somehow lost the top two buttons on her blouse. In the resulting gap, he saw the light-colored lacy outline of her bra as well as the swells of smooth flesh beneath it....

Just as quickly, he caught himself. This wasn't the time to speculate on that subject. Still, the mind's computer worked at lightning speed, and his managed to input the fact that everything looked real nice in that department....

His M-16 combat-ready, Lyons strained his senses for any sign of the enemy.

Nothing happened.

Nobody shot. No sound reached their ears. Their eyes probed for any sign of hostiles in the twilight. Once, Lyons thought he heard something. It could have been a rock dislodged, kicked loose by a careless boot.

Or it could have been the roaring of the blood in his own ears.

Behind them, about fifty yards away, was a jagged outcropping of boulders. It lay in the opposite direction from the original landing site and the hostile fire—an ideal source of cover.

"Ironman!" It was Gadgets who hissed the name.

"Yeah."

"Let's fall back, man. To those rocks."

"Yeah, okay." Lyons glanced at the outcropping and started to move in that direction. He didn't run, but just started to ease toward the boulders.

For some reason something didn't seem right.

The others started to follow him. After ten yards or so, moving silently and tensely in the darkness, every nerve straining, Lyons came to a halt.

"What is it? Why are you stopping?" It was Dana's hushed whisper, urgent and tense.

The Ironman started to speak. "I don't know. I just—"

His words were cut short by sudden gunfire that erupted from the direction of the original landing site.

They could see the orange flames from the muzzle-flashes and hear the hammering of the weapons being fired in the fully automatic mode. Simultaneously the clanging of projectiles against steel reached them as the bullets hit the chopper.

"Let's go!" snapped Dana urgently.

"No!" Lyons's voice cut like a whip.

"Come on," she began again. Lyons, however, tackled her and hauled her roughly to the ground. The other two had already dropped and rolled in opposite directions, seeking at least partial cover from even the small chunks of rock. Moments later Gadgets, who had separated himself from the others by some twenty feet, fired an answering burst at the attackers.

The staccato hammering of autoburn in short bursts engulfed them, followed by the whine of ricochets into the darkness.

As he brought his own weapon to bear, part of Lyons's mind tried to analyze why the rocky outcropping seemed to be a "no go."

At first glance it looked like the perfect cover. It was within reach probably, given the near darkness. It extended off to the side in either direction; that would give them the ability to circle back toward the original touchdown site. With luck they could come up on the ambushers.

And, to top it off, until they'd hit the dirt and Gadgets had begun to return fire, the hostiles—whoever they were—hadn't zeroed in on them. Most of the rounds had struck the chopper, now some ten yards away.

That might not be much, especially when you're talking three thousand feet per second, but it was still a hell of a lot better than it could be.

Why, then, did his instincts say no when the objective factors said, "Hell, yes"?

He was also aware that off to the other side, away from Gadgets, Blancanales had begun firing short bursts of autoburn. At almost the same moment, Lyons's ears picked out the distinctive metallic clink that signified Gadgets had burned through a clip. Politician was taking up the slack nicely.

The sound of yet another M-16 told him that Dana had gotten into the act, too.

Good girl.

"Ironman!" Gadgets low voice somehow cut through the sound of the rifles.

"Yo!"

"Shall we go for it?"

Lyons knew he was referring to the outcropping behind them.

"No! Negative!"

"Why not?" Immediately after he had spoken, Gadgets began firing again.

Suddenly Lyons had it. The reason that had eluded him leaped into his mind, a combination of sixth sense and subconscious reasoning.

The outcropping was *too* obvious. It was too logical a place to go for cover.

It was no good because it was too good.

In a flash all the pieces fell into place. And they all said no.

Sure it was getting dark, but it wasn't that dark, not pitch-black, anyway. The chopper was, after all, on the crest of a ridge. Anybody who was in position, for as long as these hostiles were, would surely have picked out their targets by now.

And yet they hadn't. Or it looked as if they hadn't. Most of the bullets were still hitting the chopper. The hostiles could well have been circling the rocky outcropping, moving toward Able Team, in the seemingly interminable period that the warriors had crouched there in the darkness before the shooting had started.

Lyons remembered the sound he'd heard—or thought he'd heard—as they had moved silently away from the downed bird.

And, to top it all off, given the muzzle-flashes from Able Team's return fire, surely the hostiles would have found their position by now. And yet nothing was coming within range of them.

It was a setup, a trap.

Somebody was trying to herd them toward the outcropping behind them. His instinct had told him that, and now his mind understood it.

The reason why they were being herded, of course, still eluded him.

"Pol!" Lyons snapped.

"¿Sí, amigo?"

"You got anything that goes bang? Like a grenade?"

Seconds later the ground shook as Blancanales let his actions be his answer.

"Now!" Lyons was up and sprinting.

He didn't run backward toward the rocks. Instead, he charged straight off to his left, downhill, taking great leaps in the darkness, heading for the shelter of a rocky gorge.

The other three followed. Moments later the rise near the fallen chopper was vacant.

In the shelter of their minicanyon, the four commandos caught their breath and hastily collected their wits.

"Nice of you to make up your alleged mind," commented Gadgets between gasps.

"What do you mean?"

"Well, while you were deciding whether to run or die, I went to town and had a couple of beers. Plenty of time."

"It's good for you," retorted the Ironman.

"Why didn't we just dash for those rocks?" Dana whispered, a decided note of anger in her voice. "You hotshots weren't standing half-naked out there like I was."

"Better you than him," said Blancanales. "At least from the spectator's view," he added, glancing at Dana's cleavage.

She shot him a withering glance but didn't respond. Lyons explained his reasoning. When he had finished, Blancanales nodded. "I felt the same way," he said, "but I didn't know why. You know?"

"Yeah." Lyons nodded. "And there's another thing, too. Back when the shooting first started, they seemed to only want to take the pilots out. That's where the gunfire was concentrated."

"Why would they just want that?" Dana's voice was hushed. "I mean, if they were going to ambush us and steal the money, why wouldn't they just kill us all?"

"Good question," Lyons muttered. "But I think I know the answer."

The others looked at him.

"They were driving us into a trap, all right. But it wasn't to kill us. Sounds like their orders are the same as ours."

"What do you mean?" inquired Blancanales.

"Simple. Somebody wants us alive. And I bet it ain't the marauders."

"Who, then?" asked Dana, her breath slowly returning to normal.

"Russians probably." As he recalled the man in their hotel room, Lyons realized that had to be it, regardless of Brognola's educated guess that they wouldn't be involved. Blancanales and Gadgets nodded their agreement.

"So what shall we do?" inquired Dana. Her voice was taut, showing tension but no panic.

Good girl, thought Lyons again. Sounds like she has guts as well as a great body. Smart, too, but then he'd worked with many women who were his equal.

"I have a plan."

The others looked at him.

"Shoot," said Gadgets.

Lyons grinned. "That's basically it. Fuck the orders to take 'em alive. We're not dealing with a bunch of asshole terrorists now—marauders, to use the Chief's word. We've got a skilled group of Commie commandos on our hands, and I don't want to think about what it'll be like if they do happen to capture any of us."

"So?" Gadgets's voice was even. "What's the plan?"

"Attack 'em. Kill the fuckers. Wipe 'em out. Once they're out of the way, we'll go after the marauders. And, if it's convenient, we'll capture them."

"And if it *isn't* convenient?"

"We'll kill them, too. Any objections?"

Nobody objected.

22

They spread out and moved forward in single file. Lyons gestured for Blancanales to lead the way. Politician was the jungle warfare expert, and although the desert was the farthest thing possible from a jungle, the same skills served him here as well.

He moved like a shadow in the desert night.

Three minutes later he held up his hand, signaling a stop. They froze and listened.

The sounds of the night settled around them. The only light was from the glittering blanket of stars and, off on the horizon, the glow of a moon about to rise above the mountains. Far away a coyote howled mournfully. A night bird made a screeching sound. Then, gradually, the more subtle noises emerged, the occasional rustle of small animals on the sand or through the stunted brush.

And there was something else as well.

At first they felt it more than heard it or saw it. Ultimately the sense that finally alerted them was smell.

The odor of man. The scent of a trap. The smell of death.

Blancanales slowly turned in the darkness. Then, just as slowly, he lifted his hand and indicated the direction of the human enemy. Politician indicated the position by pointing just ahead and to the right with his index finger, making a motion in the shape of an arc.

The others saw his signal, barely visible in the night glow. Gadgets nodded and gave a thumbs-up sign.

Slowly Blancanales's hand disappeared into the pouch he carried. Just as slowly it emerged, holding a baseball-sized object. He transferred it to his left hand, then removed a second such item from the pouch.

Training and instinct took over. Gadgets, Lyons and Dana automatically touched the selector switches on their M-16s—full-auto was the order of the day.

Politician dropped his right arm by his hip, behind his right buttock. Then he swung it upward as he lobbed the fragmentation grenade over the rise. An instant later the movement was repeated as he hooked the second one after the first.

White light flashed in front of them, and the ground shook with the force of the blast. Moments later the second blast erupted.

"Now!" Politician commanded.

Lyons and Gadgets scrambled forward. Blancanales and Dana spread out to either side.

The grenades had done most of the work that needed doing. Two men lay sprawled and mangled, past being a threat to anybody. A third man lay on his side, on his hip, still moving.

He struggled to bring his assault rifle up.

Lyons and Gadgets fired at the same time. Two short but accurate bursts flipped the soldier over and over in the desert sand.

For a few moments it seemed ultrasilent, as though the rude blasts had shattered the desert's own sounds.

Then they heard something else.

"Over there!" Lyons pointed up some ten or fifteen yards away. A man was scrabbling up the ridge. Lyons fired a quick burst and saw it miss, hitting beneath and to one side of the man.

"Shit!" The Ironman twisted the empty clip out of his M-16 and slapped in a fresh one.

Gadgets fired also, a longer sweep of bullets that stitched a deadly line up the ridge toward the soldier.

A single yell told them that at least one of the projectiles had hit, but the yell was one of sharp pain rather than mortal wound. Then the figure disappeared over the crest.

Moments later a grenade arced toward them, originating from the spot where the man had disappeared.

It was sheer luck that Lyons happened to see it. The stars made a bright blanket of glowing dust in the black night sky. Still, their light was relatively weak. But the moon, in its first quarter, was just beginning to appear above the horizon ahead of them.

By the barest of chances, the grenade just happened to loop across the yellow backdrop of the moon itself.

"Hit the dirt!"

Four bodies fell like stones and hugged the earth, faces turned down and away, muscles braced. For what seemed like hours nothing happened. Then the ground shook with the blast.

Dirt and fragments stung Lyons, and then he was on his feet and charging ahead. He crested the rise and dived forward, going over and down, ready to shoot anything that moved.

The man was getting ready to lob a second grenade.

From the way the soldier stood, Lyons could tell the man was wounded. Still, the guy was quite capable of tossing grenades over the rise until his arm got tired or he ran out of them. Or until Lyons did something to call a halt to the program.

The Ironman fired a quick burst from the M-16 as he dived forward.

Most of them missed, but a couple didn't. One of them shattered the soldier's forearm. The impact of the high-velocity bullet shattered the bone, and the incompressible blood transmitted the shock by hydrostatic pressure throughout the man's body, stunning him. The grenade fell to his feet and detonated, cutting his lower body to ribbons in a ghastly personalized display of pyrotechnic destruction.

For just an instant Lyons froze. Though he was no stranger to violent and messy death, the odd circumstances of this soldier's demise slowed him for a moment.

It was a moment too long.

Far off to his right, some forty yards up a slight rise, stood the remnants of the stone house. Gunfire erupted from that direction, and even as he began to take evasive action, scrambling forward and rolling down the gorge, Lyons knew he was going to take a hit.

He did.

The pain was both paralyzing and electrifying, and it spun him over and over down the rocky slope.

A cry tore from his throat. Then, in a mindless fury of pain and outrage, he struggled to a sitting position, elbows on his knees, M-16 at his shoulder, and autoburned the entire remaining two-thirds or so of the clip toward the source of the shots.

Agonizing pain overwhelmed him at the same moment the weapon locked open and empty. With what could only be described as a shriek, he heaved himself onto his side, his fingers frantically trying to replace the clip both for survival and to take his mind off the wound.

Then the pain subsided a little, and the next moment Blancanales was there, bending over him.

The former Black Beret was all pro—no time or breath wasted with any are-you-okays. As Gadgets would later observe, "We figured that if Carl had been okay, he wouldn't have been squealing like a stuck goddamn pig."

"Where is it, amigo?" Blancanales demanded urgently.

Lyons pointed.

"Where?" persisted Politician.

"Goddamn it! Can't you see, you blind idiot?" growled the Ironman. "I've been shot in the ass!"

"I hope the bullet didn't hit your head, too," Blancanales muttered, relief flooding over him.

Blancanales unceremoniously hauled down his partner's camou fatigues to inspect the damage.

Sure enough, the wound was a "through-and-through" on the right cheek. It looked like a neat .22 caliber tunnel that had drilled its way in from the right side just aft of the hipbone. It had exited maybe four inches farther back, at what might be termed the crest of the rise, viewed from the side.

Or to put it another way, the exit wound was at the zenith of the azimuth, so to speak. The damage, however, appeared confined to the right gluteus maximus.

"Shit, that hurts!" Lyons muttered between clenched teeth.

Blancanales chuckled. "It ought to, amigo. You got drilled but good. And your glute's nothing but muscle and nerves and fat, so it's not surprising you feel, uh, some discomfort, as they say." He hesitated, then grinned, white teeth flashing in the darkness. "Look on the bright side, amigo."

"What bright side is that?"

"At least it didn't hit, uh, more to the front. Toward the bow, so to speak. Could have shot off the family jewels. I realize that target would be pretty small, of course."

"Stick it up your ass," Lyons snarled, in a not altogether appropriate choice of words. At that moment, Dana and Gadgets ran up, keeping low to stay out of the line of fire.

"What is it?" gasped the Able Team genius. "Is it bad?"

"Real bad," said Blancanales, suppressing a grin.

"Oh, Jesus," said Gadgets reverently. "Is he going to make it?"

"I think—" Politician's intended humorous reply was chopped short by the unmistakable soft, pyrotechnic sound that could only be one thing.

"Damn! Flares!" snapped Gadgets. Moments later the desert landscape—and Lyons's untanned buttocks—were bathed in brilliant white light.

Lyons thought he heard a decidedly feminine snort of laughter from Dana's direction. Just then, however, the gunfire began again, and there was no more time to worry about a painful but not immediately fatal flesh wound.

"Fuck it!" the Ironman bellowed. Seemingly not in the least impeded by his dropped trousers he dived for cover with the others.

The flare seemed to last for an eternity. Heavy sustained fire came from the old stone homestead, and there was nothing to do but wait it out. The light started to fade at last, but even as it did so, the sound of another flare reached their ears.

We're done for, Lyons thought, raising his head and firing half a clip at the stone house.

Then fate intervened in the form of a dud flare. The missile glowed yellow but never properly ignited.

All four of them had realized they were goners if another flare went up. The enemy could simply pin them down with sustained fire while one or two of their number slipped around to the side. They could get real comfy and take their time shooting the sitting—or lying—ducks.

"Haul ass!" yelled Lyons. He gritted his teeth and drove up like a sprinter coming off the blocks.

"Take your own advice, Ironman!" quipped Gadgets, then he, too, was off and running.

Nobody had to be told what to do. They acted in unison, spreading out in a fan-shaped formation and making a recklessly headlong charge under momentary cover of darkness.

Lyons churned up the rocky slope, his powerful legs moving like pistons driven by alternating bursts of explosive muscle power. And with each step, it felt as if a miniature frag grenade were exploding a mixture of acid and ground glass into his right glute.

A ragged grunt of pain issued from his throat at every stride.

In true Ironman style, he made the hurt fuel his determination, not sap it. By the time he drew near the stone house, he was—to put it mildly—in a violent rage.

Another flare thudded into light just as he neared the structure. This time, however, it helped rather than threatened them.

The tumbledown walls of the old structure loomed before Lyons as he forged ahead, a surging machine of adrenaline, pain and rage.

Though it was probably some three feet high, he went over the breach in the lowest place, like a hurdler in the Olympics, almost without altering his stride. He landed inside, his feet scrambling for stability, and burned off the rest of the clip from the .223.

The din was thunderous in the relatively confined area, and ricochets and chips of granite flew everywhere. Then his gun locked open and empty yet again, and he twisted out the clip. As he fumbled for another, a man emerged behind the wall to his right.

The Ironman swung to face the threat as he inserted the clip.

No!

It couldn't be!

His mind refused to accept the data. It didn't compute. Input error. No way.

The clip wouldn't go in, probably because Lyons the pro had made the unforgivable—and usually fatal—mistake of letting his conscious mind distract from what should have been the automatic, second-nature act of reloading.

The stark white light of the flare made the man clearly visible.

Immense. Hairy. Fat, but the fat-on-top-of-muscle kind of fat. Hard fat.

Tattoos, a twisted tangle of snakes, running down the man's arms. Mean little pig-eyes that burned in the fleshy face.

In his hands he held a MAC-10 submachine gun. It looked like a toy in his clumsy paws.

It can't be! Lyons thought again.

But it was.

The buffalo next door to Gene's gym, the one whom Lyons had welcomed to the "insurance business" after crashing through his door with a cylinder head "search warrant." The guy whose dope Lyons had scattered into the dirt. The guy whom Lyons had threatened to kill if he ever saw him again.

A look of recognition crossed the man's face.

"Well, well, well!" he rumbled with a cruel grin. "What the fuck do we have here?"

He steadied the MAC-10 in his hands and pointed it at the Ironman's chest.

23

Ex-cop and ex-con stared at each other. Then the buffalo started to kill the Ironman.

It was something you sensed, Lyons knew. The man's eyes changed a little. Perhaps the muscles of the right forearm moved slightly as the fist tightened to pull the trigger. In less than a second, firing pin would hit primer, and Lyons's death would begin.

In a single, swift motion, Lyons grabbed a fist-sized chunk of granite from the ground and hurled it sidearm at the man.

The rock, moving at the speed of a respectable fastball, crunched against the muzzle of the MAC-10, deflecting it upward.

But not before orange flame leaped from its muzzle.

Lyons felt the hit to his body. His head snapped to one side, while his body absorbed the impact full on. Almost as if he were outside his own body—a spectator of his own battle to the death—Lyons saw his consciousness shut down to the most basic level.

Survival.

He followed the rock he had hurled, driving forward in a hard tackle. His butt was on fire, his blood flamed, and he hit the man with a bone-jarring smash.

The impact drove simultaneous grunts of effort from the two men. Then the Ironman's hands were on the weapon, and he twisted it free from the huge hands. Rather than turn it on the big man, however, Lyons hurled the gun behind him. The part of him that was outside his body, the spectator part, wondered why he hadn't tried to shoot the big man with the MAC-10.

It almost seemed as if he didn't know what a gun was, or how to use it anymore, thought the spectator.

The two men struggled in the fading light of the flare.

Lyons knew that if the buffalo got him in a bear hug, it would be all over. The other man apparently thought the same thing and clawed in closer.

Lyons danced back and hit him. He hit with three quick, hard shots, left, right, left, exploding with all the power in his body to drive the blows home. The buffalo's body shook from the blows, and then his arms were around Lyons and the pressure began.

Behind them came other sounds of mortal combat, shots and shouted commands, and a single, long, drawn-out scream.

Those sounds faded out of the Ironman's consciousness. A steel band encircled his body, and it clamped inexorably tighter, crushing Lyon's head into the sweaty chest.

His right hand found the man's jaw. Lyons drove the heel of his hand upward, a short, jarring blow that struck the buffalo along the lower shank of his jawbone on the left side.

Lyons felt the bone give, break and dislocate.

The pressure around his body began to increase a hundredfold as pain drove the man wild.

"Oh, God!" Lyons moaned. Blood roared in his ears. His head pounded until he thought his temples would blast outward.

He fumbled with his right hand, gouging in the meaty neck, looking for the carotid artery that took blood to the brain. If he could find the spot and hit it, spasm the artery or bulb it, keep the pressure on, the man would have to black out, a variation of the old "shock and lock" technique he had learned as a cop.

Where were the others? his mind screamed. Are they dead? Are my friends all dead?

Am I dead? What am I?

Then he found what he thought was the spot. He drove his right fist upward, leading with the middle knuckle of his middle finger.

Nothing happened.

He drove two more quick blows at the same spot. Then suddenly the big man stiffened, and the pressure on Lyons's spine slackened.

With the frenzy of a drowning man, Lyons fought backward from the huge beast. The man staggered away and fell to the ground.

Lyons's conscious, twentieth-century mind no longer controlled him. This was the most primitive of human emotion, mortal combat where one would live and one would die, a throwback to when man was truly an animal, living—or dying—by the strength of his body and the savagery of his primitive soul.

He leaped foward like a wildcat to attack rather than draw back.

His hands found a rock. It was hard and rough and about twice the size of his fist. A weapon. A perfect weapon. The only weapon that existed. The only weapon he needed. The only one he would ever need.

And with that primitive tool, the Ironman killed the buffalo, crushing his skull with repeated blows, growling with rage and effort and an atavistic fury, hearing the crunch of bone, feeling the warmth of blood and something that was thicker, gooier than blood, and still hitting again and again and again....

EPILOGUE

Lyons opened his eyes. All he saw was blue-green.

Blue-green walls. Blue-green ceiling. Blue-green everywhere he looked.

I know that color, he thought. That's the color of hospital walls and surgical gowns.

And morgues.

Then Brognola was there, leaning over him, saying something.

Is he identifying the body? Lyons wondered. Better ask him and find out.

"Chief?"

Brognola didn't seem to hear. In fact, he had straightened up and was saying something over his shoulder. Maybe this was the morgue, after all.

Try a little harder this time. "Chief?"

The figure turned toward him. "Carl! So good of you to wake up."

Whew! Lyons thought. It's a hospital, not a morgue. If it had been a morgue, I'd be dead. But if it's a hospital, I'm alive.

Lyons had to know.

"Did—" His lips were too dry to speak. He tried again. "Did we get them?"

Brognola grinned. It was a great grin, Lyons decided, the kind of grin that makes you want to be alive. "You got them, Ironman. You got the marauders. You also got your-self shot in the gut and in the ass, but you got them.''

"How about . . ."

"The others are fine."

Lyons closed his eyes. Mission accomplished. Now he could live. He wanted to live again. Life was where it was at.

Brognola was speaking again. "We got the plans back. And the money. And you got seven Ruskies thrown in for good measure."

Lyons tried to smile. It was hard work, and he closed his eyes again.

"Hey, Ironman."

He looked up. It was Brognola again. He was still grin-ning. "Only thing is, you didn't take them alive, the way I asked you to."

Was he angry? Lyons wondered. Disappointed?

No. That wasn't it. He must have been joking. Yes, that was it. Joking.

The Ironman remembered the phrase Gadgets had used. It was the perfect answer.

"Close enough for government work, boss."

SuperBolan #8

AN EAGLE FOR THE KILLING

A covert clique within the U.S. military is set to launch an all-out war in Central America. This secret cabal of generals believes the American people are being betrayed by a soft U.S. government. Their idea is to stage another "Vietnam." But this time on America's doorstep.

There's only one way that Washington can neutralize these superpatriots: pit it's supersoldier against the very men who trained him!

SB8

TAKE 'EM NOW

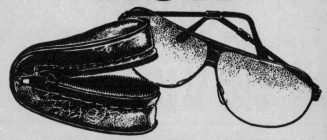

FOLDING SUNGLASSES
FROM GOLD EAGLE

Mean up your act with these tough, street-smart shades. Practical, too, because they fold 3 times into a handy, zip-up polyurethane pouch that fits neatly into your pocket. Rugged metal frame. Scratch-resistant acrylic lenses. Best of all, they can be yours for only $6.99. MAIL ORDER TODAY.

Send your name, address, and zip code, along with a check or money order for just $6.99 + .75¢ for postage and handling (for a total of $7.74) payable to Gold Eagle Reader Service, a division of Worldwide Library. New York and Arizona residents please add applicable sales tax.

Remove from pouch...

unfold once...

unfold twice...

and they're ready to wear.

GOLD EAGLE

Gold Eagle Reader Service
901 Fuhrmann Blvd.
P.O. Box 1325
Buffalo, N.Y. 14240-1325

Offer not available in Canada.

GFS1-RRR